CW01379011

DEEPING FEN

by

Rex Merchant

Dedicated To
My Mother
(A Cowbit girl.)

Copyright © Rex Merchant 2011
ISBN 9781902474 243

All rights reserved. No part of this book may be reproduced or stored in an information retrieval system other than short extracts for review purposes or cross reference, without the express permission of the Publisher given in writing.

Published by Rex Merchant
@ Norman Cottage
89 West Rd
Oakham
Rutland LE15 6LT. UK.

British Library Cataloguing - in - Publication Data.
A catalogue record of this book is available from the British Library.

Typeset, printed and bound by Rex Merchant @ Norman Cottage.

Cover designed by Rex Merchant. Fen painting by Erica Merchant.

All characters in this publication are fictitious and any resemblance to real persons, living or dead, is purely coincidental.

DEEPING FEN

by

Rex Merchant

Published by
Rex Merchant @ Norman Cottage

South Lincolnshire

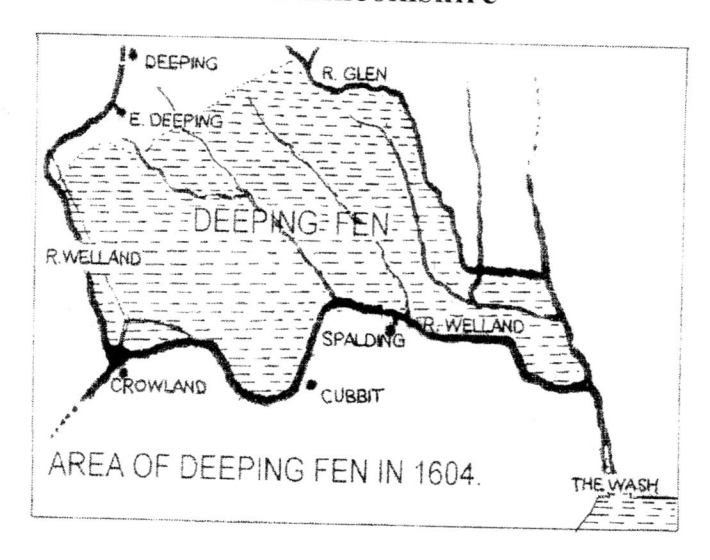

AREA OF DEEPING FEN IN 1604.

Author's notes.

Deeping Fen in South Lincolnshire was a vast area of marsh and fen bordered by the River Welland and the River Glen. The whole area flooded every winter. It was a haven for fish, especially eels, and for wildfowl of all types. The slodgers, the local fen men, fished and trapped this bountiful natural resource.

Attempts were made in Queen Elizabeth I time to raise a tax to drain the 30,000 acre fen but it proved impossible to tax the locals.

When King James came to the throne of England in 1603 another attempt was made to drain the area. Thomas Lovell, an adventurer with experience in land drainage on the continent, undertook to use his personal fortune of some £12,000 to drain the area. In return it was agreed he would be granted 10,000 acres of the new arable land.

The local slodgers, men from the Deepings and from villages such as Cubbit, realising they would be without the means to feed their families and earn a living, were opposed to these plans. Riots broke out when they tried to pull down all of Lovell's work.

Chapter One.

Molly Kettle stood in her back room stirring her latest brew of opium beer. The widow's mongrel bitch lay at her feet. The wind moaned and whistled through the sparsely thatched roof of the shack, mimicking the cries of the water birds that lived on the nearby marshes and mingling with the low murmurs of the voices of men drinking in the other room. It was the January of 1593, and the hamlet of Cubbit in the South Lincolnshire fens was dark and cold, held firmly in the grip of winter. Outside, it was a moonless night with no stars penetrating the low cloud cover. The dirt alleyways between the sparse dwellings were completely dark with only the faintest glimmer of light leaking through the cracks in a few of the cottage doors and shutters as the inhabitants huddled around their turf fires. Most sober folk were early to their beds.

Molly stirred the brew pan and sprinkled in another handful of dried poppy heads and stalks. Opium beer was a popular drink in the fen villages, taken mainly for its medicinal properties. The locals grew the white poppies on the marshes and used them to make beer to alleviate the symptoms of the marsh fever, the ague that was endemic in the fens.

The widow's dog whimpered, stood up and paced the floor, its ears straining to hear sounds that old Molly's ears couldn't detect.

"S'only the wind, ya silly bitch! Lay down." Molly ordered, but her dog ignored her and stayed alert, its nose sniffing the air and its tail up. As it moved purposefully towards the back doorway, a sudden gust of wind moaned through the ill fitting door. The dog barked, its hackles raised, its eyes fixed on the door.

"Stupid dog!" The old lady took a swipe at the animal with the wooden paddle she used for the brew but the dog easily dodged the blow.

Molly was about to aim another at it when a deep male voice called from the other room.

"Bring more beer, Molly".

Molly filled a stoneware jug from a barrel and took it to the men. The dog was still guarding the door when she returned to the brew room. Molly softened her voice. "I've told you, there's nothing there but the wind, you silly bitch." As she bent down to the dog to pat and reassure it, her head almost touched the back door; it was only then she heard a faint cry coming from outside. She hesitated and put her ear closer to the door, not sure if it was the wind, a bird disturbed in the night or someone calling out. The cry came again and it sounded human! She realised there could be someone out in the night who needed help.

Throwing open the door, Molly peered out into the darkness. The faint glow from the room, lit only by a rush light, illuminated the dirt track for a few feet from the cottage but the rest of the roadway was in total darkness. As her eyes grew accustomed to the dark she saw the outline of a shadowy bundle in the road. Grabbing the rush light from its iron bracket, she held it aloft and stood in the doorway. There was definitely something unusual out there, several paces from her shack. Suddenly, the wind increased and blew out the spluttering flame. She stood silhouetted in the open doorway; in total darkness but for the faint glimmer of light issuing from the other room behind her. Molly was unsure what to do, but her dog brushed past her legs and ran to the bundle, whimpering and barking low in its throat. Then a faint human cry reached her ears.

"Is someone there?" She raised her free hand to shield her eyes and peered into the gloom. A louder cry answered her and the shadowy figure of a small girl sat upright in the road. Molly took a hesitant step onto the roadway. "Annie? Annie is that you?"

The girl shouted back then broke into deep sobs.

Molly ran out to the figure and knelt down beside her.

"I...I've...been...set upon" The girl managed to explain between sobs.

Molly, whose eyes were getting used to the dark, could see the girl's clothes were dishevelled; her skirts were pulled up to her chest, revealing her bare legs and stomach. Hastily she pulled the skirts down to make her decent and helped Annie get onto her feet and stagger to the brew house doorway.

"Come in lass. Sit down." Molly guided the girl to a stool set in the corner, and shouted to the three men who were drinking in the other room.

"What's up, Molly? Run out of beer?" One of the group joked as he peered through the doorway into the dark brewing room.

Molly took the smouldering rush light into the main room and lit it. As she carried it back into the brew room and placed it in the wall bracket, they could all see Annie, sitting and sobbing in the corner.

"It's little Annie Owen. I just found her on the road outside. She says she's been attacked."

The three men crowded into the small room and surrounded the girl, their bulky figures filling the restricted space.

"Attacked? Here in Cubbit? Never! Who did it, Annie?"

Molly pushed them back. "Give her some room. She'll tell us soon enough."

Annie's sobs slowly subsided. She dried her eyes on the hem of her soiled dress.

"Well?" Molly prompted.

"I was coming to get my dad... "

"He's gone home already." One of men interrupted her.

"Shut up!" Molly chided. "Let the girl speak."

"I was coming to get my dad, and someone jumped on me in the dark." She started crying again.

Molly patted her on the shoulder to soothe her. She shook her head sadly and looked helplessly at the men. "Someone has taken advantage of the lass and she's only twelve."

"Taken advantage?" The most drunk of the three men repeated the words as if he didn't understand them.

"Raped her!" Molly exclaimed. "Her clothes were yanked up over her head and she has blood on her dress and her legs. She's been raped!"

Everyone in Cubbit knew Annie. Her father, Charlie Owen, was a regular drinker at the brew house since his wife had died. His only child, Annie, had stepped into her mother's place and struggled to run the home for him, but he spent all his time drinking and mourning his late wife.

"My God! Rape? Here in Cubbit? Who would do such a thing?" The men who were rapidly sobering up at this news, were getting increasingly angry at the thought. Bert Ward, the local marsh reeve, a large man with a loud voice, turned to Annie. "Who was it? Who did this to ya?"

She wiped her eyes and shook her head. "I didn't see. He ran up from behind and pulled my clothes over my head and pushed me to the ground. I tried to struggle but he was too heavy and too strong."

"He could still be out there!" Bert exclaimed.

"Aye, maybe." Molly agreed, casting worried looks at the back door.

"Let's search the village." Bert made for the door, followed by his two companions.

"I'll see you home, lass." Molly grabbed a shawl, threw it over her shoulders and put a rope lead on her dog. Taking up a stout stick for protection, she helped Annie rise from her stool. They all spilled out into the night on their various missions.

Charlie Owen's home was a one-roomed shack where he lived with his daughter. It was not far from the brew house, set beside the Spalding road on the very edge of the village. When Annie pushed open the door she found Charlie fast asleep on the floor where he had collapsed. His loud snoring and his foul breath testament to the amount of beer he had consumed that evening.

Molly aimed a kick at the prone figure but couldn't rouse him. Her dog sniffed at his face then backed away. Molly started to shake the drunk by his shoulder to rouse him.

"Don't." Annie begged her. "Let him sleep. There's nothing he can do in that state." She threw herself onto a bed of dried rushes in the corner of the room and curled up, her tear stained face turned to the wall."

Molly understood the girl's reaction. Charlie Owen drank at her brew house most nights and he could be violent when he'd had too much to drink. "I'll leave you to sleep, lass. I'd better get back to my own place." She closed the door and hurried back to her home, peering nervously into the darkness as she went, knowing that someone had attacked a young girl and he could still be roaming the village.

When Molly got back to the brew house, a commotion was in full swing. She rushed into her front room attracted by the men's shouts. There she found them holding a young lad from the village. She immediately recognised the boy from his flaming red hair and the long, tattered, blue coat he was wearing. It was the village simpleton, Peter Small. That coat was never off his back since a passing stranger had taken pity on him one cold January morning and thrown the worn out garment to him.

"We caught him skulking on the high bank." Bert Ward explained. "He won't tell us what he's been up to, or why he's roaming out on a cold night like this."

Peter struggled to get loose from his captures but they held him firmly. The boy was in his early teens, simple minded and crippled from birth. He could hardly speak and spent his days begging at the roadside.

"He won't tell you because he can't." Molly said. "Peter's not normal. He's a simpleton. He's weak in the head. He was born a cripple with no wits. Let him go."

"Did you attack Annie Owen?" Bert Ward ignored Molly's advice and insisted on questioning the lad.

Peter struggled and made strange animal noises but there was no coherent answer.

"I think he did it." One of the other men asserted. "I think he did it. I've seen him sitting by the roadside watching the women go by, and he was the only one out and about tonight when no honest man would be."

"Aye, so he was." Bert agreed. "We ain't got proof enough for the court at Spalding but we can make sure he never does it again. You've got a daughter, Dick, what do you think?"

"Too right Bert. Let's sort it. Let's cut out his stones." Dick pulled a lambing knife from his pocket. The blade gleamed bright in the light from the rush lights.

Molly listened to this exchange with growing horror. She was powerless to stop the men who seemed determined to take some sort of revenge on the lad. She rushed out of the house and ran to Peter's home where his widowed mother was already asleep on her bed.

By the time the two women got back to the brew house it was too late. The boy had been castrated.

Across the village, in the Owen's shack, Charlie Owen still lay on the floor, snoring loudly in his drunken stupor, completely oblivious to his daughter's pain.

Little Annie lay on her bed facing the wall, lonely and frightened, crying herself to sleep.

Chapter Two

By the spring Annie Owen knew she was pregnant. Living close to nature as she did in the fens she was fully aware of the signs. Her periods stopped and her belly began to swell. At three months she begged Molly Kettle to tell her how to end the pregnancy and get rid of the unwanted baby growing inside her. Her father spent his days fishing and trapping and his nights drinking at the brew house. He seemed indifferent or blind to his daughter's predicament and would not discuss it with her.

One spring morning Annie walked to the brew house to ask Molly Kettle's advice. "You must help me. How do I get rid of this?" She pointed to her stomach.

Molly was a worldly old woman and had seen many of the village women in similar straits but none so young or so needy as little Annie.

"It's dangerous to abort a child," she told her. "But if you really insist, there's a herbal woman over at Crowland who might help. It'll cost ya though."

Annie shook her head. "Dad drinks all the money away these days. I haven't a penny to call my own."

Molly, who took most of Charlie Owen's money for her beer, felt beholden to the child. She patted Annie on the shoulder. "I'll try and sort it out for you, lass. I'll send a message to Crowland and get you the potion."

Annie looked nervous at the thought of taking a medicine.

"It's only mugwort." Molly assured her. " It a herb that grows on the river banks, but it's made into a draught for you to drink. It don't always work mind you, but I have known it loosen a child in the early months."

Annie thanked Molly and went back home to her work.

Some days later Molly Kettle called on Annie when her father was away trapping eels in the fen. She gave the girl a dark glass bottle of mugwort juice and instructions how to take it.

"Drink it down in one go, Annie. You'll need some water after it as it tastes foul."

"What happens then?" Annie asked, nervously.

"If it works you'll have heavy courses and lose the baby. You'll have to rest for a day or two but you should be alright. If you want me, send for me." Molly left the shack by the Spalding road and walked back to her own home leaving the girl holding the dark glass bottle and pondering on what to do.

Annie turned the bottle around in her fingers, watching the thick brown liquid inside it. There were bubbles and bits of vegetation floating in the potion, making it look dark and sinister. The girl hid the medicine in her straw bedding and got on with her chores and with weaving the eel traps she fashioned from willow wands.

That night, after her father had returned from the brew house and was snoring loudly on his bed she retrieved the bottle of potion and crept out into the yard. There, by the light of a full moon, she drank the whole bottle in one go, following it with a long draught of water from a bucket in the yard. The potion taken, she crept back to her bed and tried to sleep.

Next morning Annie felt ill. As the day progressed she became worse with violent stomach pains and continual vomiting. She was too ill to contact Molly Kettle and just curled up on the floor clutching her stomach. By that evening, when her father returned for his evening meal, the girl was too ill to rise from her bed.

"You've got a stomach affliction. "He told her. "Stay in bed and you'll feel better tomorrow." He left her alone in the hut and went for his nightly fill of beer.

Molly Kettle, who had been half expecting a call from Annie, asked Charlie Owen how his daughter was.

"She's fine. She's been sick and she has a stomach ache. Probably eaten something she shouldn't have."

Molly didn't continue the questioning but suspected the girl had taken the potion already. She determined to call on Annie the very next day when her father was out on the fen.

By the next morning, when Molly called, Annie had stopped vomiting but had had a show of blood like a light period. The girl looked deathly pale and so weak she was hardly able to rise from her bed.

"Has it worked?" She asked the old lady.

Molly looked at the blood loss and shook her head. "That's no child," she told Annie. "The mugwort hasn't worked for you."

Annie shook her head and burst into tears. "What can I do now?"

"Nothing. You look as if your own health is suffering. Any more potions and you might die, let alone the unborn child. It looks as if God means you have this one, Annie."

The girl broke into deeper sobs and buried her face in her bed.

After her initial reluctance to bear a child, Annie resigned herself to her fate and stoically got on with her life. She cooked and cleaned for her father and made the eel traps and fishing nets he needed for his work. She became so good at this work, several of the other fen slodgers started buying their traps and nets from her. This small income she hid to buy clothes for her unborn child.

Charlie Owen made no comment about her increasing size and the imminent birth of his grandchild. He himself was beginning to show signs of failing health with the early symptoms of the fen ague, that raging fever that attacked most of the fen people as they grew older. As the fevers and shivering fits grew more frequent he turned to the only thing that eased the condition; the opium beer that Molly Kettle brewed especially for it. Each evening he would return from working the fen, eat his supper and then go to Molly Kettle's to pass the night drinking. By the time he rolled home, drunk and tired, Annie was fast asleep from exhaustion. Charlie fell onto his bed and slept soundly like someone already dead.

By the late autumn Annie was at full term. When she went into labour two of the village women came to her hut to help with the delivery. She was still only thirteen and only a slip of a child but the baby, a boy, was born alive. The birth was a difficult one but the midwives knew their craft and saved both mother and child. Annie was exhausted but held her hands out for her son.

"He's a tiny boy, Annie. I don't give him much chance my dear but you love him while you can." The old woman had seen such tiny mites before and knew the chances of survival were slim.

Annie took the baby in her arms and hugged him to her. "Is there anything else wrong with him?" She asked as the two women stood whispering to each other and avoiding her gaze.

"He has a club foot."

Annie touched the baby's legs and ran her hand over his feet. She felt his tiny right foot was deformed and twisted. She hugged him even closer to her breast and talked softly to him to comfort him.

The new born boy was not expected to live as he was so small and sickly. He was christened Toby when he was only a few days old at the small thatched church in Cubbit as he was not expected to thrive.

When the news of Annie's delivery spread through the village the fact that the baby had a club foot did not go unnoticed.

"Stands to reason he takes after his sire." Bert Ward, the village reeve, told everyone drinking in Molly Kettle's parlour. "Stands to reason and only confirms what we know already. That idiot, Peter Small, is his father, you mark my words."

Peter Small who was a cripple, had been shunned by some of the villagers since the evening of the rape, but the news of baby Toby's club foot confirmed his guilt in the eyes of most of the villagers. Whenever they left their home, he and his mother were spat on by the local children and called names. The children chanted their hate at him.

"Peter Small. Peter Small. He ain't got no sense at all..."

They pelted him and his mother with mud and stones and drove them indoors whenever they were seen begging on the roads near the village. Eventually, one morning, the village awoke to find them gone.

Molly was walking her dog that morning and was one of the first to miss Mrs Small and her son. She hesitated at the smouldering ruin where their hut had stood only the night before. She could see the wooden house and its meagre contents had burned to ashes. All that remained was a blackened patch of earth and a stone hearth.

"Funny business." She told her dog. "Been no mention of moving, and I spoke to Mrs Small only two days ago when we walked past here. That's a mystery."

Mystery or not, the hut where Peter and his mother had lived for years, had been burned to the ground and there was no sign of either of them.

The fen reeve, expressed most of the local's feelings in the ale house that night. "Good riddance to 'em. They've taken to the highways to beg for a living, I'll be bound. We don't want the likes of 'em here."

When Charlie Owen came home from the ale house, a little more sober than usual, he told his daughter the news. "Seems Peter Small and his mother have left the village. Their hut is burned down and they've gone. Folk say they have taken to the open road to beg for a living."

Annie felt sorry for the boy and his mother. She had always insisted Peter was not her assailant on that winter night. She tucked her baby in beside her and said a silent prayer for the Smalls that night in the privacy of her bed.

Chapter Three.

Ten years passed and England had changed for ever. Good Queen Bess, who had ruled for 45 years, died in 1603. She was the last of the proud Tudor line. James Stuart, King of Scotland, ascended to the English throne that year and the two kingdoms became one.

Against the odds, Toby Owen had grown into a lively ten year old, small for his age but bright enough. His limp slowed him down but it didn't stop him leading an active life. He helped his mother weave the willow eel traps and the string nets that she made to earn their living. The boy had survived thanks to Annie's care and attention. Much to the surprise of the rest of the village, Charlie Owen accepted the child and treated him as one of his family. Toby grew up in Cubbit helping his mother and grandfather.

By this time, Charlie Owen, a fen slodger who fished for eels in the rivers and trapped birds on the marshes to keep his family, had fallen ill with the ague. Charlie took to his bed when the symptoms were worse and treated his fevers with copious draughts of opium beer. Gradually, as the disease progressed, he worked less and less and was finally confined to his bed, unable to fend for himself or his family. His young daughter, Annie, struggled to eke out a meagre living for the three of them. She had never been a bonny girl but now she weighed so little and looked worn out with worry and work.

Life in the village of Cubbit carried on as it always had. Men fished and trapped on the streams and marshes of the Deeping Fen. Little altered in the village until the Owens awoke one morning to find they had a new neighbour.

It was early in the month of March. Jake Fowler, a young man recently returned from the war in Ireland, was building himself a one-roomed hut on a flat area of land where a shack had previously stood. The site was just a few score yards from the Owen's home.

Toby, with the curiosity of youth, hobbled along the road to greet the newcomer.

"You going to live here, close by us?" The boy asked.

Jake eyed the small lad up and down, noting the club foot and his thin appearance. He stopped laying the stone foundations, smiled at the boy and mopped his sweating brow. "Yes. Whose asking?"

"I'm Toby...Toby Owen. But why live here? Why here?"

Jake looked at the heap of rubble almost hidden by coarse grasses and the levelled area where a hut had once stood. "Because I used to live here a long time ago."

Jake had been born in Cubbit and spent his early years there. When, in his teens, both his parents succumbed to the marsh fever, and he was left alone, he had gone to London and joined the private army of Robert Devereux, the Earl of Essex. His duties took him to Ireland in the abortive attempt to quell Tyrone's Rebellion but he had been wounded there. That wound and the effect it had on him, put an end to his army career. After several years serving his noble master, he gave up the army life and returned to his native fens to the outdoor life he'd enjoyed as a boy. It seemed natural for him to seek out a familiar place and a familiar way to earn his keep, trapping wildfowl and fishing on the marshes and fens as he had in his youth.

"Can I help you?" Toby asked.

"Perhaps you can." Jake said. "I need some hurdles to build the walls. Do you know who weaves willow hurdles in Cubbit these days?"

"My mum."

"Oh! That's convenient. Where can I find the lady?"

The boy pointed to his home, just along the Spalding road. "There".

Jake finished digging up the last of the stones that remained from the solid base of his old home and laid them out anew as a square foundation for his walls. He made sure he unearthed every one of the remaining sandstone pieces as they were a useful commodity, rarely found in the fen silt. Toby sat on the grass beside him and chatted happily to his new friend.

By mid morning, Jake had reused all the stones he could find and had finished his preparations. He stopped to drink from his water flask, wiped his mouth with the back of his hand and turned to the boy.

"I think you'd better take me to your mother now, so I can order some woven hurdles for my walls."

At the Owen's shack, Annie was sitting cross-legged on the floor weaving a willow eel trap. Toby rushed into the room and threw his arms around her.

"I wondered where you'd gone." Annie told him. "Your grandpa needs some more opium beer, he's pretty bad this morning. I want you to go to old Ma Kettle's. I wish you wouldn't wander off when I need you."

Jake who had followed the boy into the hut stood silent and unnoticed in the doorway. Once his eyes had become accustomed to the poor light in there, he glanced around the room. The walls were hung with willow eel traps, in preparation for the new season in late March. Newly woven fishing net lay in a heap in one corner. There was a bed of hay piled against one wall with a large man noisily sleeping on it. Finally his gaze settled on the young woman sitting on the floor. She was small framed and thin, hardly taller than her son.

He noticed especially that she had a mass of dark curls tied back with string. Jake cleared his throat noisily to let the woman know he was there.

Annie stood up, flustered by the arrival of a stranger in her home. Toby grinned happily. "This is Jake. He's our new neighbour."

The girl frowned and looked the stranger over. Cubbit was a close community with few incomers and strangers were regarded with some suspicion.

Jake held out his hand. "Jake Fowler. My family used to live in a hut just along the road from you. You probably won't remember me because I left the area some years ago. I've come back to Cubbit to live and I'm rebuilding the old home."

"He needs some hurdles to make his walls, mum. I told him you wove them."

Annie dropped her wary attitude and smiled a welcome. "Sorry I didn't know you. I may have been too young to remember your folks but I do recall hearing the name. My Dad..." She nodded at the figure lying noisily asleep on the far side of the room, his laboured breathing rasping loudly. "He may remember you."

"Owen...Charlie Owen, isn't it? My parents knew him well." He looked at the girl and raised his eyebrows. "Marsh fever?" He asked in a low voice.

"Yes, the ague". She whispered.

"I lost both of my parents to it before I left the village." Sadly he shook his head. The young couple stood in silence, not knowing what else to say to each other.

Finally Jake broke the silence and abruptly changed the subject. "Now, about these hurdles. And I'll need some rushes for my roof."

17

Annie led her visitor outside to the area behind the hut where she had a stack of woven hurdles standing against the wall.

"These are all I have. I weave them for the sheep farmers on the marshes. There are some made of hazel but mostly they're willow. I can't help you with the rushes but I know that Bert Ward, the fen reeve, has plenty in his yard from last season."

Jake eyed the collection of hurdles and chose six that were the sizes he needed. "Can you spare this many?"

"Surely. I can always make some more."

The area at the back of Annie's hut was a shambles, a jumble of old eel traps, broken nets and bundles of willow wands waiting to be woven into new traps. Among this debris Jake noticed the prow of a small boat sticking out from under a heap of thicker willow sticks. He picked his way through the jumble and hauled out six of the hurdles for his building project.

Having agreed a price and paid Annie for them, Jake, with a little help from his new friend Toby, carried the hurdles to the site of his new hut. All that day Jake worked to erect the four walls and the roof of his shack. He tied the hurdles together at the corners with willow wands woven tightly into them and fixed two of the hurdles to the top of the walls to make a frame for a pointed roof. Toby helped when he wasn't busy helping his mother. By nightfall, Jake had bought several bundles of dried reeds from the reeve, carried them through the village to his site and made a thatched roof to keep the hut dry. He had a rainproof roof and he had the framework of his four walls fixed in place, but these were still bare hurdles and provided him with no barrier to the wind.

"You going to sleep here tonight?" Toby asked.

"Yes."

The boy pulled a face at the thought.

"Don't worry about me." Jake laughed. "In my army days I've slept in far worse places than this, and in far more dangerous ones. I have my backpack as a pillow and my coat to keep me warm. Anyway, by tomorrow night I will have the mud walls completed and it will be wind proof. Now all I need is a fire to cook my supper and to keep me warm for the night."

Toby eyed the lumpy backpack doubtfully. "You'll have to take that long stick out before you sleep on that."

Jake looked sharply at the lad and back at his pack. "Aye... my stick... Must keep that safe... I might need it." His friendly manner seemed to change when the boy took an interest in his bundle of belongings. "I think it's about time you went home." He said gruffly.

Toby reluctantly returned home to his mother dragging his club foot and dawdling all the way.

Jake built a fire from some dead sticks and dry grasses and lit it with the sparks from his flint and steel. As the sun set over the fens and daylight began to fail he huddled up closer to the fire and cooked a bird on a spit over the embers. When darkness fell and he had eaten, he lay on the grass. He checked the contents of his pack, taking out the old matchlock gun that Toby had mistaken for a stick and hid it under a pile of dried grass against his back. With his head resting on the roll of his meagre belongings as a pillow, he curled up with his back towards the cold March winds and slept fitfully that night, memories of his recent hand to hand fighting in Ireland and the shoulder wound he had suffered there, haunting his dreams.

Next morning Jake awoke at first light. He had a busy day planned getting his hut walls sealed with mud. He collected damp clay and dried grass from the marsh and piled it behind his hut waiting to be worked. By the time Toby appeared, Jake was treading the cob mixture with his bare feet, working the grasses into the clay to strengthen it.

"Uh! That's a mucky job!" Toby pulled a face as he noticed the wet mud oozing between Jake's toes.

"Mucky but necessary." Jake stopped his constant trampling to take a rest and gulp a drink from his water bottle. By mid morning he had prepared enough of the clay mixture to start filling the gaps in the willow hurdles. Taking the mud mixture in both hands he threw it at the hurdles, forcing it into the spaces between the woven branches. This treatment soon stopped the gaps that the wind found and strengthened the walls.

Toby eventually tired of watching Jake treading the clay and made his way back home to help his mother.

Jake continued working steadily until late that afternoon, when he had filled the entire four walls with the first layer of clay and grass. He knew the cob mixture would need to dry out before he could add further layers to it but he now had windproof walls and a waterproof thatched roof. It was looking much more like a home. He was pleased with his progress.

Jake stopped work while there was still some daylight remaining and walked across the marsh to wash the clay from his body in a small pool of clear water. He could have carried on filling the walls but he had another pressing job to do. He realised the firearm he had hidden in his backpack needed a more permanent hiding place. The old matchlock gun was one taken from an enemy casualty on the battlefield in Ireland; it was the very gun that had fired a ball into his own shoulder.

In the heat of battle, Jake had managed to ignore his wound and had attacked his assailant with his sword. His first blow broke the fuse holder of the gun; the next thrust chopped the man down. The gun was damaged and wouldn't fire but Jake reckoned it was repairable. He was sure a firearm would be a useful asset to a wildfowler on the marshes but he also knew it was valuable and would be a target for thieves if he left it on view in his hut, for there were very few such expensive weapons in the fens at that time. He doubted if there was another firearm in use on the Cubbit marsh as the locals were too poor to own one. Mindful of the innocent interest already shown by Toby, he decided to dig a pit in his hut floor and conceal the gun properly until he could get it repaired and back in working order.

Using his knife, Jake dug a hole in the soil floor of the hut under his sleeping area. He hid in that cavity, the gun, a powder horn and a shot mould, wrapped in part of an old blanket to protect them. He covered it all with a thin layer of willow branches and dry soil and placed his bedding on top. That task completed, Jake lit a fire against the evening chill and ate a simple meal of stale bread and dry cheese, which he'd saved in his back pack.

Chapter Four

The next morning when Jake had eaten the remainder of the cheese and bread for his breakfast, he knew he must leave the work on his hut and walk into Spalding to get some essential supplies. Bread was baked and beer was brewed in Cubbit but little else was available unless you caught it for yourself. Once he started fishing the rivers regularly and trapping wildfowl he would have little need to buy food, but until he became self sufficient he had no choice but to buy his provisions. He realised the mud walls of his hut were still far from dry and hard. There was no chance of adding more clay to them until that happened, so he had time to spare.

There were several other reasons Jake knew he must make a trip to Spalding, the nearest market town. He needed fishing line and hooks. He also needed to get the broken matchlock firearm repaired. He knew there would be blacksmiths in the town who might tackle that delicate job, he also hoped there would be sellers of black powder and lead shot, both vital supplies if he intended to use the gun to hunt wildfowl.

With his matchlock gun wrapped in sacking and hidden in his backpack he set out to walk the two three to Spalding. It was market day when he arrived at the great stone bridge spanning the Welland river. The town was bustling with traders and the river was alive with boats of all sorts and sizes. Beside the river, near the docks, he found the blacksmith's workshop. He had to wait some time to see the craftsman as there was a stream of customers wanting his attention. Finally he managed to speak with the man.

"Can you repair the serpentine on a broken matchlock gun?" Jake asked in a low voice, not wishing to draw undue attention to himself. Matchlock firearms were not plentiful in the fens and could be the target for thieves.

"I haven't ever made one." The smith observed. "But I dare say I can if you have a pattern for it."

Jake pulled the firearm from his back pack and handed it to the man. "The end that holds the fuse has broken off. You can see what's needed from the remaining part."

"Aye, just a small piece of steel to grip the fuse. Shouldn't be a problem." He eyed the young man curiously, noting his dusty clothes and worn boots. "Yours is it?" He turned the gun over in his hands, noting the initials JF carved into the wooden stock

Jake smiled. "Yes, those are my initials. The gun's mine, captured from an Irish soldier in Tyrone's rebellion. I did my time fighting for the crown under Robert Devereux."

The smith slapped Jake on the back in a good natured way. "Sorry, man, just checking it's your property. We don't see many firearms in this area. Things like that usually belong to the gentry."

Jake nodded he understood. "Now, when can I pick it up. How long will it take you to repair it for me?"

"This afternoon if you like, and if you can pay me for the work."

"Good. I have other business in Spalding that will take me some time. ..Tell me, who sells black powder and shot in the town these days?"

"Only one man. Johnny Acres. He lives down by the Westlode."

Jake thanked the man and left to find Johnny Acres premises. As he turned to leave the smithy he bumped into Bert Ward, the fen reeve from Cubbit, the man who had supplied him with the reeds for his roof.

"Hello again!" Bert greeted the young man. "What brings you to the big city?"

Jake grinned. Spalding was hardly London, but compared with Cubbit it was quite metropolitan. "Just getting some provisions."

"You've come to the right place then. I come from here. My brother is the baker in the Market Place. Tell him I recommended you to him." Ward shouted after Jake as the young man left the smithy.

At Acres' workshop Jake managed to purchase some black powder and some lead to make shot but there was no saltpetre fuse in stock.

"Leave it a day or two and I'll get some more made." Johnny promised.

With the supplies ordered for his gun, Jake made his way to the market place to buy bread, cheese and some freshly caught herrings. He made a detour to the far side of the town to call at the ropewalk for some rope and a quantity of thin cord for making fine nets. His errands done, he made his way to the docks where he sat and ate his lunch and watched the boats being loaded and unloaded.

Spalding was a bustling little port; part of the port of Boston, but very busy in it's own right with its own customs office and a thriving trade with London and the near continent. Sheep fleeces and leather skins were traded from the town and luxury goods like cloth, wine and olive oil were brought in. By the time Jake had finished his lunch he felt it was time to check on the progress of his matchlock gun.

As luck would have it, the blacksmith was just quenching the new steel serpentine in oil to harden it, when Jake arrived at the smithy. It took only a few minutes for the new part to be riveted onto the gunstock and tested. Jake, who was familiar with the mechanism, having fired similar guns in battle, checked that the trigger pushed the new serpentine onto the powder pan to fire the charge of black powder. He tried it several times. Satisfied with the repair he said. "Good. You can add gunsmith to your skills now. How much am I in your debt?"

Having paid the man, he wrapped up the gun and secreted it in his backpack before he set out for Cubbit and his new home.

The Spalding road was not busy that afternoon. Only a few people passed Jake as he walked the three miles back to Cubbit, but as he approached the village he came face to face with a large group of horsemen. Judging by their rich clothes, their plumed hats and expensive leather boots, it was an important and wealthy group. The quality of their mounts and the number of retainers with them surprised him. Few men could afford such luxuries. Jake watched them with interest as they approached him on their way towards Spalding. Because of the number of horse and riders involved, Jake stepped off the roadway to let them pass him by, but they halted close by and proceeded to look out over the marshes, looking towards the river Welland and Crowland. There was a lot of pointing of fingers and heated talk about the area. Men and horses wheeled around in the road, the riders talking animatedly to each other. It looked to be a serious business the men were discussing. Jake could not hear what they were saying but they showed a great interest in the Cubbit marsh and the view towards the river and over the fen.

As he waited at the roadside, Bert Ward caught up with him and stood at his side. After a few more minutes of heated discussion the horsemen regrouped and galloped off towards Spalding.

"What was that all about?" Jake asked his companion.

"I don't know." Bert stroked his chin thoughtfully. "But I can tell you it must be important because that fellow in the red coat is Sir John Gamlyn, the local member of parliament. He doesn't waste his time on trivial things."

Jake looked at his companion and raised his eyebrows in surprise. "An important man indeed. Must be something special for him to ride out here."

"Aye, I would say so. He lives the other side of Spalding, at Fulney Hall. We don't often see him this way. I wonder what they were doing here?"

Jake shrugged his shoulders. Who knew what the gentry were up to? Whatever it was it didn't concern him. The two men continued their journey home, walking side by side towards Cubbit

"Did you get your firearm repaired?" Bert suddenly asked, taking Jake by surprise with the direct question. Jake had noticed the reeve at the smithy in Spalding but didn't realise the man had taken such an interest in his business.

"Aye." Jake answered very briefly.

"Used to guns are you?" Bert persisted in his interest in the matchlock gun.

"Yes, you could say that. I was with the Earl of Essex's men in Ireland, quelling the rebellion. I've fired them a time or two."

"Ah! That explains it. An army man. And used to firearms. You told me you'd moved here when you bought those reeds. Am I right in thinking you might be wanting to use that gun to shoot wildfowl in the fens?"

"Maybe." Jake was cagey about his plans, not being sure why Bert was so interested in them.

His companion explained his interest. "I'm the fen reeve for Cubbit."

"I know."

"And I have to uphold the rules. Did you know there's no taking of fowl from Lady Day to Whitsuntide on the marshes?"

"I know...that's from the end of this month to mid May, while the fowl are breeding."

"You've come at a difficult time of year if you were banking on feeding yourself from the marshes."

"Well, on the Feast of the Annunciation, in late March, the eel fishing season starts, so there'll be plenty to keep me busy and plenty of fish to catch."

Bert looked surprised that his young companion was so familiar with the local fen rules.

Jake smiled. "You won't know me because you weren't living in Cubbit when I was a young lad, but I was born here and brought up here by my folk. I lived here before I joined the army. I spent my youth wildfowling and fishing on these marshes."

Bert smiled. "That explains it, you're local. I wondered why you chose to make your home here…by the way…did those reeds do for your roof?"

"Fine" Jake nodded, knowing full well the question was unnecessary as the man would have seen the progress on the hut as he walked to Spalding earlier in the day. There was something about the reeve he didn't trust.

As they came to the outskirts of the village the two men parted company; Jake went to his partly built hut and the Bert Ward carried on through the village to his own home.

Once in the privacy of his own four walls, Jake checked the matchlock gun again, setting the serpentine against the spring and pulling the trigger to gently release it. Satisfied it would function properly he wrapped it in a sack and hid it under his bed once more, then he walked the short distance to Annie's hut to buy a small hurdle to serve as a door for his home. With interest shown in his business from young Toby and now Bert Ward, he felt he needed to make his home more private.

Chapter Five

Once Lady Day had passed, the eel fishing season was underway but Jake needed traps to take advantage of it. He had been mulling over some plans for a few days, ideas that would help him and hopefully help Annie. He admired the girl for trying to keep her family fed by her hard work and realised she could help him get re-established on the fens. He felt his plans could be advantageous to both of them and they would each gain from the arrangement. One morning in late March he approached his neighbour with a proposition.

"Annie, I need a boat to work the fens. I can't set eel traps and fish if I can't get onto the water. I know I could make myself a coracle, given time, but I noticed you have an old boat buried under the bundles of willow withies at the back of your home. Is it sound?"

The girl shook her head. "I really don't know. Dad used to use it but it's been out there in the weather and not used for some time. You can pull it out and take a look if you like but there's a lot of willow bundles piled on it as we only harvested them last month."

Jake followed her outside and lifted the willow bundles off the old boat. It took some time to clear the area as there was a whole season's stock of willow wands to move. Once it was uncovered completely, he could see the boat was a flat bottomed punt, ideal for navigating the shallow waters of the fens.

Toby, who had just returned from Molly Kettle's, joined them in the yard. He was excited when he saw what was happening. "That's granddad's boat. Can we launch it on the river, mum? I'd love to sail in it."

Annie looked askance at her son and shook her head. "There's no way you are going to use this boat on the fen until we are sure it's sound. It's been out here for ages and probably leaks like one of my eel traps."

Jake turned the punt over to shake the soil and debris out of it. When he turned it back upright he noticed a pair of wooden stilts had dropped out of it. "Ah! Another useful tool; stilts. Boats can't get you over soft mud but stilts can."

Toby picked up the stilts and tried to climb onto them.

"What about the boat?" Annie asked. "Is it river worthy?"

Jake stood the punt on its end, held it against the light and searched for holes and cracks in the woodwork. Satisfied he could see non, he lowered the punt down again. "I'll have to carry it to the river to try it, to be sure it doesn't leak, but it looks sound enough. Lets go inside, Annie, I want to make a suggestion to you that I hope will be a help to both of us."

While Toby played outside with the stilts, Jake and the girl went inside to discuss his ideas.

Jake came straight to the point. "I was thinking that I will need nets and eel traps to catch fish, and you make them. You also own a punt and stilts, which would make it easier to get to the furthest and more inaccessible parts of the fen to catch even more. If I share my catch with you, will you supply me with the things I need?"

Annie thought for a few minutes then smiled and answered without hesitation. "Of course. I'm sure my dad wont have any objections to you using the boat as he's not able to use it himself now. I can certainly supply the eel traps and fishing nets and I can meet the kedger and sell your catch for you as I'm here all day working. If we can share the rewards it should work out just fine for both of us. Let's give it a try and see."

Later that day, with Toby's help, Jake carried the punt and the stilts across the marsh to the open water. He launched it slowly into the shallow water at the river's edge to check it was sound. Luckily the punt had survived unharmed under the protective covering of willow branches. It floated without any signs of a leak. Jake held the boat steady while Toby clambered into it, then stepped in and pushed off from the shore using one of the stilts.

Toby was very excited to be on the river. He wriggled on his seat and nearly capsized the boat.

"Sit still!" Jake shouted at the boy. "I don't wish to get wet today."

Toby quietened down and sat very still while Jake poled the boat across the river and back again.

"Well, Toby, that proves the old punt is river worthy, now we must carry it back home and sort out some traps and nets. I'll also need a proper pole to push the boat in shallow water and a paddle to navigate the deeper parts of the river. We'd better look out for suitable branches on the willows as we make our way back home over the marsh."

When they'd returned to Annie's hut and delivered the punt back safely, Jake and Toby went inside to tell the girl the good news.

"The boat is fine." Jake explained. "I will be able to go further into the fen and catch more. We will have a lot more to sell to the kedger when he calls."

Annie was pleased with the news. Life could be a little easier for her and her family if the arrangement with Jake worked out. She stopped him as he made to leave the hut.

"I was hoping to speak with you about something else, Jake." She seemed hesitant and unsure when she spoke. He stopped in the doorway, smiled reassuringly and encouraged her to continue.

Annie blurted out her request. "Would you take Toby with you sometimes and teach him the skills he needs to work the fens?"

Jake didn't answer immediately. Trapping fish and wildfowl on the marshes was a solitary job. The fewer people involved, the less noise and disturbance would be made. Often he would have to wait for hours in silence to net the waders, ducks or geese. Toby was a nice enough lad but judging by his experience on the river he might be more of a hindrance than a help. At last he spoke. "I'll have to think about that, Annie. I'm used to working alone and in silence."

Toby who had been watching and listening to the conversation could contain himself no longer. "Will ya take me with ya Jake? I want to learn about eeling and wildfowling. I promise I'll do as ya tell me." Youthful enthusiasm showed in his voice.

Jake reconsidered his reply. Annie had been more than generous allowing him to use the boat and supplying eel traps for free. He broke into a smile and slapped the lad on the back. "Yes Toby we'll give it a go. But you'll have to do exactly what I tell you or we'll get nothing and then we'll all starve."

Toby grinned from ear to ear and hugged his mother.

That evening Jake sat by his fire carving a new paddle from a willow bough. It had been a fruitful day for him. The arrangements they had agreed, should help them all in the future. He was pleased with himself, for most of the fishermen in the village made their own traps or got them from Annie and paid her for them, but his would be free because he would share his catch with her. She would deal with the wagons from Spalding, selling the kedger the eels, fish and fowl that he had caught. That freed him to spend more time fishing and wildfowling. It was an arrangement that suited them both. It also brought him into regular contact with her, for he was beginning to enjoy her company and the arrangement they had made would ensure he saw her most days.

Chapter Six

Thomas Lovell halted his horse at the gates of Fulney Hall, the home of Sir John Gamlyn, and admired the old building. In the morning sunlight the Barnack Rag sandstone glowed golden yellow beneath its crown of new thatch. He knew a little of the history of the house, which stood on the eastern edge of Spalding on the Holbeach road. The stone had been reclaimed from the priory at Spalding at the dissolution of the monasteries. It was of the highest quality as befitted Sir John, the local Member of Parliament. The Hall was a house to be proud of; the sort of house Thomas aspired to own, one day when he'd made his fortune.

He loosed the reins and allowed the horse to walk slowly down the driveway towards the main entrance. The sound of his approach brought a stable boy running out to greet him. Thomas dismounted and handed the reins of his horse to the lad.

"See he gets watered lad. I have a meeting with your master."

The boy hurried off, leading the horse to the stables at the back of the house. Thomas beat the grime of the journey from his yellow surcoat and breeches, slapped the side of his boots to remove the loose dirt from them and took off his hat, hitting it against his thigh to clean it. The dust from his journey rose into the still morning air. Satisfied he was presentable, he presented himself at the house.

Inside Fulney Hall, Sir John Gamlyn sat at an oak table surrounded by documents. He rose as soon as Lovell was shown into his study.

"Thomas. Good to see you again. I hope you had a good journey here."

The visitor bowed his head, acknowledging the greeting. "I got your message, Sir John. I came as soon as I could."

Sir John Gamlyn was a powerful man in the Spalding area. He was one of the largest land owners and, more importantly for Lovell, he was responsible for the survey of the Deeping Fen, that vast area of flooded land between the River Glen and the River Welland, which would pay handsomely for being drained and turned into useful, productive, farmland.

Lovell, who had some experience of land drainage on the continent, was hoping to be given the right to drain that fen. He knew King James was keen on the project and he also knew the King's Council had failed to raise the necessary taxes to pay for the scheme. It was common knowledge that they had tried in 1600 to get the scheme started when the old queen was still alive. They had passed a Drainage Act but it was not until 1603 when they tried to tax the local fen people to pay for the work, they realised the futility of their undertaking. Everyone knew how independent the fen folk could be and few were surprised when the money was not forthcoming. Now Lovell had a proposal of his own to put to Sir John; one he hoped would get a favourable response.

"Sit down, Thomas." Sir John indicated a carver chair drawn up to his table. "I have here the plan of the Deeping Fen. It covers over 30,000 acres of land. But of course you will know all of this already, a man with your experience in land drainage."

Lovell smiled. He knew Sir John and the crown needed him as much as he had need of them. He felt he was the only person capable and willing to undertake the work. He cleared his throat.

"You have a proposal, I understand." Sir John prompted.

"Yes Sir. I will undertake to drain the whole of Deeping Fen at my own expense for a fair portion of the reclaimed land."

Sir John nodded and smiled encouragement. This was what he had hoped to hear; this was the only way the impecunious crown could get the work done.

"I will put my personal fortune and my expertise to work for the King on this project but I expect a goodly recompense in return."

"The Court of Sewers met locally only recently. I have here the papers drawn up all ready for you to sign when we have filled in the details." Sir John spread his hands over the documents on the table. "What do you regard as a fair recompense?"

Lovell nervously cleared his throat again. "I will undertake the drainage and embankment for a third portion of the reclaimed land."

John Gamlyn looked down at the scattered documents, averting his gaze to hide the smile of satisfaction that flitted momentarily over his face. He nodded slowly and studied the plans, appearing to be giving the offer deep consideration.

Lovell repeated his offer, misreading the other's hesitation. "I have £12,000 at my disposal. I will accept no less than one third part of the new land."

Sir John turned towards his visitor, a serious look on his face. "I think we can persuade Chief Justice Popham to accept your terms but you must hear our terms first." He hesitated while he glanced down at the parchment he had taken up in his hand. "The Court of Sewers met at Deeping recently. Their chairman, Lord Burleigh, insists you will undertake this task solely at your own expense and you will complete it within a period of five years. In return we can agree that you will be granted a third of the reclaimed land; that would be about 10,000 acres by their reckoning."

Lovell smiled and let out a sigh of relief. With his experience he would need a lot less than five years. "I accept your terms."

"Good man!" Sir John rose from his carver chair, strode around the table and slapped Lovell enthusiastically on his shoulder. "The King is in a hurry to get this land into production. I myself have put aside money to buy some of it from him." He walked back to his chair and sat down again opposite his guest. "Now we must sign the undertaking to make it binding and legal. I will get my clerk to take the agreement and write in the details we have discussed. Will you take a glass of wine while we wait?"

Thomas Lovell accepted the wine with a beaming smile. He had come to Fulney Hall to drive a hard bargain for the drainage of the Deeping Fen and he was of the opinion he had done just that.

As they sipped their wine, to pass the time while they waited on his clerk, Sir John questioned his visitor about the plans for the newly drained land. "I suppose the land will grow barley, wheat and rye once it's drained properly. At the present time it is only used to fatten cattle and sheep over the summer months. The locals fish and trap eels and wildfowl during the winter."

"That land will be very productive. There's no better soil than reclaimed fen and marshland. Think of all that goodness put into it by hundreds of years of rotting vegetation."

"Quite so. But what about the salt from the inundation of sea water?"

Lovell smiled. "Within a year or two all the salt is leached out of the soil."

"I know you have much experience of drainage schemes abroad on the continent. Tell me, what will it actually entail?"

Lovell sat back, toyed with his wine glass and expounded on his favourite subject. "The secret is to dig new dykes to drain the water from the low lying areas. Then that water is put into the rivers. This is done by using wind driven pumps to raise the dyke water to the level of the main river."

Sir John nodded he understood. "I suppose you'll have to build up the Welland banks to contain all that new water and dredge the river bed to keep the channel clear?"

"The new banks need to be ten to fifteen feet higher than the old ones and we will put sluice gates where the dykes feed the river so there will be no flooding back at times of high tides. We'll also have to dredge the river and build new sluice gates at the outfall of the Welland where it meets the sea, so it can discharge all the water."

Sir John nodded sagely and the two men fell into a companionable silence as they sipped the wine.

After a few minutes of silence, Sir John raised a finger to get his visitor's attention once more. "One word of caution, Thomas. There are folk who do not agree with this scheme. There are people, even in parliament, who fear the locals will be displaced from their fens and will lose their rights to fish, to catch wild fowl and dig turf for their fires. We have no desire to see more beggars on the roads. There could well be some local opposition."

Lovell shifted uncomfortably in his chair. "I had heard whispers of some opposition but surely if the King wants it, it will go ahead. As for the locals causing trouble, surely that is a matter for the local magistrates. Anyway, I will be recruiting labour in these parts and giving employment to many of the locals."

Sir John nodded vigorous agreement. "Quite so my good fellow, quite so. I was just thinking aloud and forewarning you there could be some small problems."

"I will have a hundred or more men working for me. I don't think a few dissenting locals will cause us any bother."

Sir John sat back in his chair and drained his glass. Everything seemed to be going according to his plans. When the clerk returned with the legal agreements both men signed them and each took a copy.

"I will see Chief Justice Popham gets this copy. You have yours and we have a good agreement." Sir John saw his visitor to the stables to collect his horse and watched him canter down the drive and out onto the Holbeach road. Back in his study he poured himself another glass of the excellent wine and sat back in his chair, pleased with the morning's business.

Thomas Lovell, his precious contract folded safely in his inside pocket, cantered back to Spalding and his room at the White Hart. He was already making plans to hire a hundred men and make a start on the drainage and embankment of the Deeping Fen. When he had set his overseer to recruiting labour, he was resolved to follow the River Welland three miles to the south, to the village of Cubbit, which was on the very edge of the area to be drained. He wanted to see for himself the state of the fen and the state of the river banks in that area.

Chapter Seven

In the small hours of the morning, Jake Fowler woke up with a start. It took him several minutes to accustom his eyes to the dark interior of his hut and to remember where he was. He lay back, bathed in sweat and shaking from another disturbing dream. Since the day he had been shot in a skirmish with Tyrone's followers in Ireland, he had suffered vivid flashbacks and many nights with broken sleep. He got up from his bed and took a long drink of water then went to his door and stepped out into the night. All was quiet except for the occasional sound of wildfowl disturbed on the marsh. A Redshank, put up from its resting place by a fox or an otter, cried its haunting warning into the night and flew across the marsh. A Curlew sounded its plaintiff alarm call far off in the fen. Jake relaxed and took several deep breaths of the fresh night air then returned to his bed to try and sleep until the morning.

After a poor night with hardly any sleep, disturbed by the pain in the old wound in his shoulder and the return of his terrifying nightmares, Jake went into the village looking for Molly Kettle at her brewhouse. He remembered the house from when he was a boy, when Jack and Molly Kettle brewed beer for the village. It seemed Molly was now widowed and carried on the business on her own. He knocked on her back door.

"Come in" Molly's voice shouted from within.

Jake pushed to open the door and was greeted by Molly's dog, fussing and rubbing itself against his legs.

"Bad dog! Come away." Molly aimed a blow at the dog but it dodged her easily and went to lay down in a corner of the room. She looked the man over; he was a stranger. Cubbit was a small village and she knew everybody who lived there. Strangers were few and far between.

Jake introduced himself. "Mrs Kettle, I'm Jake Fowler. My parents used to live here."

"Ah! I thought I knew you. You are the image of your dad, God rest his soul. If I remember rightly you left us soon after your parents were buried. Do call me Molly, all the village does."

Jake nodded. "I want to buy some opium beer, Molly."

The old lady eyed thoughtfully, doubt showing on her face. "You look fit enough, lad. Not got the ague, have you?"

"No! Heaven forbid!" He rubbed his damaged shoulder. " I have an old battle wound and sometimes I can't sleep for it." He handed her a drinking bottle that he'd brought back from his army days.

Molly filled the bottle and took the coins he offered her. "Back in Cubbit are you, for good?"

"I don't know about for good, but yes, I'm building a hut on the old site my parents used."

"Army was it? Where you got your wound?"

"Yes, but I've finished with that life now. Thought I'd give my old haunts a try." He turned to go.

Molly turned back to her pan of steaming brew. "Close the door securely after you, lad, or the dog'll be out."

Jake made his way back to his shack and sat on his bed while he ate a meal of bread and cheese. After the meal he took out the matchlock gun and oiled the wooden stock to stop it splitting. As he checked the action of the new fuse holder, he was interrupted by a knock on the door.

"Who's that?" He made to hide the gun.

"Toby."

Reassured, Jake leaned the firearm against the hut wall and opened the door for the boy to enter.

Toby immediately spotted the gun and rushed over to it, excitement in his voice. "A gun! I didn't know you had a gun, Jake. Will you use it to shoot duck?" The boy picked up the gun, turned towards Jake and pointed it at him.

Jake's reaction was instinctive and instantaneous. He snatched the firearm from the boy's hands and shouted at him, "Don't ever do that again! What do you think you're doing?"

Toby was shocked at this reaction. He burst into tears and ran out of the hut.

Jake pushed the matchlock gun under his bedding. His heartbeat still thumping loudly in his ears and his face coloured bright red. He broke into a cold sweat, beads of water covering his brow. He sat down on his bed breathing heavily and buried his head in his hands, shocked at his own reaction. Reaching for the bottle of opium beer he took several deep swigs from it.

After several minutes, Jake mopped the sweat from his brow and managed to control his heavy breathing. Faced with the gun like that, his old fears had returned with a vengeance; his nightmares had suddenly become a reality. He wrapped the firearm in its sacking covering, hid it in the recess under his bedding and sat down to recover his composure, but his recovery was interrupted by the sound of light footsteps and a faint tap on his door.

"Who's that?" Jake mopped his damp forehead again and pushed the cloth back in his pocket.

"It's Annie. Can I come in?"

Jake opened the door to the girl and sat back on the bed.

"Toby has come home in an awful state. He said you were mad with him and something about a gun. What's he done? I can't get any sense out of him."

Jake sighed deeply and beckoned the girl to sit beside him. "I'm sorry, Annie. I shouted at the boy when it wasn't necessary."

"What's he done this time?" Annie insisted on knowing.

Jake decided to be frank with the girl; he felt he owed it to her. "When Toby came to see me I was cleaning my gun. He picked it up and pointed it at me."

"Oh my God! You mean he could have shot you?"

"No, no! It wasn't loaded. It was perfectly safe."

Annie frowned and looked at her companion for a further explanation.

"Annie, I was shot in the shoulder when I was fighting with Robert Deveruex's men in Ireland. I was shot by an Irishman with that very gun."

Annie's eyes widened with surprise.

"You were shot? Were you hurt badly?"

"Yes, but I managed to run the bastard through with my sword before I passed out. The gun was damaged but afterwards my mates picked it up and gave it to me as a trophy."

"I'm so sorry. I suppose Toby brought back bad memories for you, pointing a gun at you like that."

"You are so right. I didn't realise how much I was affected by it."

Annie sat quietly musing what to say next. She detected the faint smell of opium beer in the air; it was an odour she was all too familiar with at her own home. She looked searchingly at Jake. "You don't have the ague, do you?"

Jake grinned. "No. I occasionally have nightmares about my army days and I can't sleep. Last night was just such a night. It's some time since I got that wound but I relive the events regularly in my dreams. That's the main reason I no longer fight for a living. I came back to the fens for a quiet life and to forget about wars."

Annie frowned. "Why keep the gun?"

Jake nodded that he completely understood her question. "I sometimes ask myself that question, but I think it's to lay the memories to rest. I feel if I can use the gun for something peaceful, like hunting wildfowl, it will take away the bad feelings I have about it."

"Have you used it to hunt?"

"Not yet. I'm working my way up to do that some day soon."

Annie got up to leave. She turned and said . "I'm sorry Toby upset you. I do hope this hasn't put you off teaching him to fish and trap eels."

Jake rose from his bed, fully recovered from his ordeal. "No. I enjoy his company. He's a good lad. He's just a typical curious boy, just like I was at his age"

Annie left Jake's hut, satisfied that all was well between him and Toby. She felt she now understood more about this newcomer to the village and was happy to let her son accompany him on the fens and marshes. She went home and tried to explain to Toby what had happened.

Chapter Eight

For the first few days out fishing in the borrowed punt, Jake decided to venture on the river alone. At first he had propelled the boat with a quant, a pole he had cut from one of the waterside willow trees, but once he had finished carving a wooden paddle he sat in the bow of the punt and used that to propel and steer it.

Toby was disappointed that he had to stay at home but his mother understood that Jake had a lot to do to familiarise himself again with the fen and the river and to learn where the best places were to set his traps and his dead lines. The marshes had altered a lot since Jake's youth. The mud banks and quick sands moved on a regular basis and could only be understood by daily contact with them. The tides from the sea and the flood water coming from inland, constantly altered the terrain. The fen slodgers lived on their wits, relying on their experience and their knowledge of the area.

At first light, Jake Fowler paddled his small boat into the middle of the river and moored it to a willow stump sticking up above the surface of the water. This was where he had set his last eel trap the previous day. He tried to pull the trap into the boat but the found he tethering rope was broken and the trap was nowhere to be seen. The muddy waters of the Welland swirled around his flat bottomed boat as he struggled to locate the woven willow trap at the bottom of the muddy river. He dragged his quant along the riverbed trying to snag the lost trap. After several minutes dredging in the mud, he located it and managed to get it onto the boat.

"Damn!" Jake cursed aloud as he examined the trap. It was empty and the narrow end of the woven willow funnel was broken away. From the look of the damage he knew something had chewed the woven willow to get at the eels trapped inside.

Jake guessed it had to be an otter that had caused the problem. There had been signs of a large dog otter on the river for a few days. Jake had noted several sprints had been left on a particular flat area of mud and he had caught a glimpse of the otter once as it swam near the river bank. On several occasions he had seen a telltale trail of bubbles as he poled his boat upriver and the animal had dived for cover at his approach

Jake loved the wildlife of his native Lincolnshire fens even though he trapped and fished for fowl and fish to feed himself and eke out a meagre living. Otters he regarded as a necessary evil, just another of God's creatures like himself, living off the rivers, the fens and the marshes, but he wasn't happy the animal had ruined one of his best eel traps.

Knowing Annie wouldn't be pleased, he shook his head at the thought of telling her, for she had only recently woven that trap for him. Then he smiled to himself as he thought of the girl, realising the broken trap would be a good excuse to spend more time talking to her.

Annie was only twenty two years old; some years younger than he was, and she was a single mother with a ten year old son but he was beginning to like the girl. Unfortunately she seemed so preoccupied with scratching a living, bringing up her son and nursing her sick father that she seldom found time to speak to him, let alone get to know him better.

Jake threw the broken trap into the bottom of the boat beside a sack of eels, still heaving with life as the fish struggled to escape. Local folklore insisted that eels would not die until sunset, even when their heads were cut off. He doubted this story but he knew their sinuous bodies still wriggled even after he had chopped their heads off and he knew in the wild they could live out of water for some time, even crawling long distances over the damp earth to get from one pool to another.

With the eel traps emptied and reset with fresh bate, Jake turned his attention to the dead lines he had set the day before. Using dead lines was an efficient way to fish a moving river. A line with several baited hooks was strung across the river and left overnight to see what would be tempted by the bait. Jake had hooked pieces of raw fish on his deadline and anchored it on wooden poles driven into the mud at each side of the river. Most of the baits had been unsuccessful, being nibbled away and eaten by fish too small to take the hooks but two of his hooks had done their job and caught two Pike. Pike were common in the fens and some grew to a fair size. Jake was lucky; one of the fish was a beauty and as long as his arm! He hauled the line out of the water and deposited the struggling Pike in the bottom of his boat. One blow on the head from the but of his pole dispatched the fish. The larger fish would fetch a good price from the kedger as Pike were regarded as a delicacy in the city. The other Pike was a smaller one but still big enough to provide a meal for four.

It had been a good day on the river. The adult silver eels were running well in the currents of the Welland and most of his traps had been full. The two Pike he had caught were an added bonus. He turned the boat for home and let it gently glide on the outgoing tide towards his mooring place opposite Cubbit church. The river had formed a sharp elbow in that area, veering towards the village and slowing down in its progression towards the sea. At that time of day the sun was getting low in the sky; its warm glow reflected on the water behind him, transforming the muddy surface into liquid gold. Dozens of small birds skimmed the surface of the river, catching the numerous flies that hovered in clouds just above the muddy water. Hundreds of wading birds were still probing the rich mud for food.

This was Jake's favourite time of day; his work was over, the catch was good and his thoughts turned to the tasty meal he would prepare when he arrived home.

Jake moored the boat at the water's edge, taking care to tie it securely lest the returning tide worked the rope loose and took the craft upriver. He secured the day's catch onto his quant and hoisted it over his shoulder. The heaviest sack, the one containing the eels, he tethered close to his back; the two Pike he tied together by their tails and hung them nearer the end. With the pole balanced on his shoulder, he picked up the damaged eel trap with his free hand and started the walk across the Cubbit marsh towards the village, the church and the roadway.

Cubbit church, with its untidy thatched roof, was one of the few landmarks visible along the earth bank, which carried the roadway that skirted the marsh. This area of low lying marshland contained the flood waters when winter came and the Welland overflowed its banks. Jake made his way towards the church knowing that Annie's cottage was nestling out of sight, just to the left of it. The shack the girl shared with her illegitimate son and her invalid father was nothing but a one roomed hovel, but even that was bigger than the home Jake had built for himself on the edge of the Spalding road.

He soon worked up a sweat walking towards the bank and the road. That spring evening was unusually warm and the air was full of flying insects, gnats and mosquitoes that thrived on the fenland marshes. The early blades of grass that would make the rich turf to fatten the cattle and sheep the locals grazed on the summer pastures of the marshes, gave off a pleasant, musty, odour as his boots crushed them.

Halfway to the church, Jake stopped to shift his load. He transferred the heavy pole to his other shoulder and took the trap in his other hand. As he rested for a minute his eyes were drawn to two horsemen riding on the top road towards Cubbit. At the church the riders stopped, dismounted and vanished from his view. After a few minutes they reappeared on their horses and seemed to be looking towards him at the marshes. As Jake neared the bank he could see them more clearly: one was a well dressed gentlemen and the other was probably his servant. They looked out of place in that poor area; certainly, they were not Cubbit men.

The horsemen vanished from Jake's view as he rounded a tall patch of reeds, growing in one of the low lying, marshy, pools. The brown plumes of the reed bed waved in the evening breeze, whispering as the leaves brushed against each other. Suddenly, a grey heron rose from the bed, flushed out by the sound of the fenman's approach. Jake watched it as it flew towards the river, its neck curled close to its body, its long legs trailing out behind it and a fat fish held firmly in its bill. As he rounded the reed bed he noticed the horsemen turn their mounts towards Spalding and canter off in that direction. Jake watched them as they gathered speed and eventually were lost to sight. He mused on what could possibly interest such fine folk in a view of the marshes, but his thoughts were cut short by a shout from the top of the bank.

"Jake!" A young boy shouted his name, waved his arms at the fenman and started to stumble down the bank towards him. Jake recognised the boy immediately from his awkward walk and from his appearance. It was Toby, Annie's young son, who always walked with an uneven gait.

Jake raised his arm holding up the broken eel trap and shouted back to the lad. "Come and give me a hand, Toby. I'm fair tired out."

The lad hobbled up to the young fenman and took the eel trap from him.

"Another damaged one?"

"'Fraid so. We have a lazy otter on the river who'd much rather take my catch than chase his own. Your mum wont be very pleased. This trap is the one she made for me only last week."

Toby put his hand under the bottom of the sack, which was swinging on the pole over Jake's shoulder, and felt the weight of the heaving bag of eels.

"Good catch, in spite of the otter. The kedger comes tomorrow to pick up the fish and eels for London. He'll be pleased with this lot. We should get a good price for them"

The kedger bought fish and fowl from the fenmen, took them to Spalding and transported them by butter boat to the higglers in the London markets. It was a busy trade that provided money for the fen slodgers and helped to feed the fast growing population of the capital city.

As Jake and Toby walked up the embankment to the road, Annie came out of her shack and stood waiting for them, her arms folded over her thin chest, her unruly dark hair blowing across her face. She frowned when she saw the damaged eel trap.

"Another one, Jake? What do you do with them?"

"Don't blame me. An otter took a fancy to my eels."

The slightly built girl took the trap from her son and led them into the hut.

Inside the single room, away from the evening sunlight, it was dark. Jake stood in the doorway letting his eyes get used to the subdued light. He glanced at the piles of willow wands that Annie used to weave the eel traps, then over at the heap of dried hay and rushes piled in one corner and the inert body of the elderly man laying on it.

"How's your father today?" He asked the question but he'd already guessed the answer.

"No change." Annie sighed. "When the kedger comes and we get paid for the eels I will have to buy more opium beer for him. His ague has got much worse these past weeks. He can't stop the shakes and he keeps going hot and cold."

Jake knew all to well the devastation caused by the ague. Men said it was the damp mists and the cold winters that brought on the freezing shakes and the hot sweats. He knew from his own experience, the effects of the illness that had killed both his parents.

With an effort, Annie shook off her melancholy mood and smiled at the young man. "Looks like we'll have a good catch to sell tomorrow. I'll add these to the barrel we have out the back." She took the heaving sack of eels and went out of the hut.

Roused by the voices, the old man raised himself on his elbows and blinked at the newcomer. He groaned and reached out for the pot of beer set on the floor by the side of his bed. Toby limped over to his grandfather and helped him hold the mug. After a deep draught of the beer, Charlie Owen seemed to regain some little strength.

"Jake? 'Tis Jake ain't it? Come over here lad."

Jake sidled over to the older man. "Aye, it's Jake."

"Had a good day, lad? Catch lots of eels?"

Jake nodded.

"By God! I wish I were out there with thee boy. But I doubt I shall work the river again."

Jake was about to protest but the old man broke into a paroxysm of coughing. Annie came back into the hut and rushed over to her father's side. "Come on dad. Lay down and save your strength."

She smiled at the old man and handed him his opium beer. Turning her face towards Jake, she frowned and sadly shook her head.

Jake looked down at his boots. He didn't know what to say in such circumstances. As a young teenager he had seen both his parents die from the ague and he knew the signs. He felt that Charlie was not long for this world.

Annie smiled at Jake again. " Will you stay and eat with us? It's only eel stew again but at least we will eat well tonight."

Jake agreed readily. He had hoped for such an invitation rather than having to prepare something for himself in his small hut along the road, and it gave him a chance to speak to the girl and maybe get to know her better. To show his appreciation he untied the brace of Pike, handed the smaller one to her and suggested. "The large one can go to the kedger with the eels tomorrow, but maybe you can cook this one for tomorrow's meal for us?"

She smiled her appreciation. "Good idea. We'll certainly get a good price for the bigger one."

The small group sat crosslegged on the reed strewn floor and ate the soup from wooden bowls. Jake was hungry from his day's work on the river and the marshes. He emptied his bowl quickly, mopping up the last of the stew with a hunk of dried bread Annie had given him and leaned back on the wattle wall of the hut.

Annie spoke first. "You had a good day, Jake. That sack of eels will please the kedger tomorrow morning. I'll split the money with you when you come back tomorrow evening."

Suddenly Charlie Owen interrupted them. He struggled to sit up coughing violently, then was sick all over himself and his bed.

Annie rushed to her father's side and propped him up. She mopped the vomit from his chest and soothed him.

Charlie grasped her arm as she did this. "You're a good wife, Gwen. I don't know what I'd do without you."

Jake stood up to leave, feeling embarrassed for the family, while Annie settled her father down again. When she had done this she walked outside with her neighbour.

"Gwen?" Jake raised his eyebrows.

"That was my mum's name." Annie explained. "Sometimes when he's delirious he mistakes me for her. People tell me I look very much like she did when she was young."

Jake nodded he understood then said his farewell. "I must go now. Lots to do before tomorrow."

Chapter Nine

Early next morning Jake was awakened by a shout at his doorway.

"Can you come, Jake. Grandpa has fallen and we can't move him. He's too heavy for mum and me to lift."

Jake instantly recognised Toby's voice and could hear the urgency in it. He got up from his bed and dressed hurriedly. Outside in the dawn light, he found Toby pacing up and down in a very agitated manner.

"Fallen has he? Let's give you a hand." He ran to the Owen's hut with Toby in slow pursuit.

When Jake arrived at Annie's hut she met him at the door and led him through to the back yard where Charlie Owen lay in a heap on the ground.

"He went out to the midden and couldn't walk back." She explained. "I can't lift him, he's too heavy, and Toby isn't much help, he's too small."

Jake bent down to check the old man and was relieved to find him still conscious but breathing heavily. He put his arm around Charlie's chest and hauled him up to a sitting position.

"Thanks...lad.." The old man wheezed.

"If I take your weight, will your legs work to walk inside?"

"Aye...let's try." Charlie struggled to get upright but finally managed it with a lot of help from Jake.

With Annie and Jake's help the old man staggered into the hut and collapse onto his bed. "Sorry lad...old legs too weak these days...to carry my own weight."

Jake smiled his reassurance. " No problem. Glad I was on hand to help."

Annie couldn't thank her neighbour enough for coming to the rescue. "I don't know what I'd have done without your help. I do hope we haven't stopped you from fishing or anything."

"No. I was just getting up and thinking of some breakfast, then I was going to suggest I took Toby with me on the fen to do some bird netting."

Toby almost danced for joy when he heard this suggestion.

Jake turned to Annie and continued. "Just one problem. I'll have to ask you if I can borrow a large net. I haven't had time to make one yet."

"That's the least I can do after your help with dad and as you're going to teach Toby how to fend for himself."

After breakfast Jake picked up the net and walked with the boy across the marsh to the boat, which was tethered on the bank of the river.

"Where are we going?" Toby asked excitedly.

"I'm aiming to net some waders this morning so we need to get right out on the fen to the mud banks towards Deeping. I want to get in place before the tide comes in so we'd better get moving."

With the punt loaded with the net, a pair of stilts, himself and the boy, Jake poled it into the centre of the river and made for the deep fen. Once they were out of sight of the Cubbit road, Jake left the main river and propelled the boat up a side stream into an area of fen covered with reed beds, alders and thick undergrowth. Toby was chattering all the time but finally Jake held his finger up to his mouth and demanded silence. "We are getting close to the mud banks where the waders feed. Complete silence from now on. I'll signal to you if I want some help."

Toby contained himself with some difficulty but he knew Jake would take no nonsense from him so he remained quiet.

When they had reached the area that he had earmarked for netting, Jake ran the boat aground into a thick patch of rushes. Using the stilts he walked through the flooded marsh carrying the net until he reached more solid ground then he went back and fetched the boy, carrying Toby on his back.

Whispering low in the boy's ear, Jake explained. "The other side of this mound there will be hundreds of waders feeding on the mud. As the tide comes in they will move nearer to us as long as they don't suspect we are here. I'm going to set the net along the shoreline so we can catch them."

Toby listened, wide eyed and excited.

Jake continued his whispered instructions. "You will take one end of the net and I'll take the other end. We mustn't move an inch or make a noise. When I give the signal we both move like lightning and cover the birds with the net. I'll raise my hand like this when the time comes."

Toby was very excited but he contained his excitement. He knew if he spoiled this outing, Jake might never take him out again.

They laid the net along the shoreline, and hid themselves in the reeds, stationed at each end of it. Jake took a dead Redshank from his pocket and propped it up with twigs to give the appearance of a live bird feeding near the net, then the hunters settled down to a long wait.

After an hour, the tide had turned and the water level crept up the mud bank towards the two hunters. The waders: Redshanks, Oystercatchers, Plovers and a few Dunlins, were busy feeding at the edge of the water. As they approached the decoy bird, Jake whistled, imitating he call of a Redshank feeding, aiming to put the quarry at its ease. Gradually the feeding birds moved nearer and nearer to the trap. Toby hardly dared to breath in case he spoiled the catch. He watched Jake intently waiting for his signal.

Jake watched the slowly approaching birds, calculating the best time to spring the trap. Suddenly he raised his hand and whispered "Now Toby!"

The boy was ready. He followed Jake's example and threw the net forward and over the feeding birds. They managed to net several score of them. Jake rushed at the net and grabbed the struggling quarry. Quickly he wrung the neck of each one and disentangled it from the netting.

"Well done, Toby. Patience has netted us at least a score of waders. It was well worth the wait."

Toby was ecstatic. His first time netting birds and they had done well. He helped Jake gather up the dead birds tying them by their legs into bundles. Jake slung the catch to the belt around his waist where they hung lifeless like a feathered apron.

"Better move on now." Jake explained. "No use waiting here any longer. We've put all the other birds to flight and they wont be back for hours."

Toby walked behind Jake to where they had left the punt. As the tide was rising fast, Jake used the stilts to get to the boat then poled it nearer to the mud bank where Toby was waiting. "If I throw you the stilts, do you think you can walk to me on your own?"

Toby nodded. He had been practising stilt walking at the back of his home.

Jake threw the stilts to the boy then watched him try to walk through the mud towards him. It wasn't an easy task as the wet mud sucked at the stilts and the lad was clumsy because of his disability, but Toby did manage it eventually.

"It's a bit more strenuous stilt walking in deep mud, isn't it." Jake sympathised. " Keep practising and you'll get stronger at it."

Toby collapsed into the bottom of the boat exhausted by his efforts.

Jake poled the boat back towards Cubbit, stopping occasionally to check his eel traps. As well as the ten brace of birds, he had caught several dozen eels in the willow traps. He emptied them into the bottom of the boat, where they wriggled about until Toby grabbed them and put them into a sack. Jake baited his traps afresh with bits of dead fish and lowered them back into the river, tying them to the wooden stakes, which he had driven into the river bed.

Once they were close to home, Jake dragged the boat up the river bank and tethered it safely. They picked up the day's catch and walked across the marsh to Cubbit where Annie had a meal waiting for them.

Charlie Owen was fast asleep on his bed and remained so all the time the family ate their meal.

"Is he alright?" Jake asked.

"Not really. He drank too much opium beer when he got back on the bed and he's been asleep all day." She hesitated, shrugged her shoulder, then continued. "At least he left me in peace to get on with net making." She indicated the pile of freshly woven netting in the corner. "With Toby out the house as well, I got a lot done. The only interruption was when the kedger called and took all your catch."

Jake grinned at this welcome news.

Annie took the pot off the fire to serve the evening meal.

Toby was full of excitement at his first day on the fens with Jake. He couldn't wait to tell his mother about the bird netting. He couldn't stand still and breathlessly explained where they had been.

"Calm down." She told him "I know exactly what you're talking about. I used to help my dad when I was your age." She smiled at Jake. "It's good to see him so enthusiastic."

Jake got up and made to leave.

"Oh! I made enough stew for all of us. Wont you eat with us?"

Jake could smell the delicious stew and was tempted to join them. "Why not? Thanks for the offer. I will join you, but I must go home first and get cleaned up."

Chapter Ten

"Fish stew?" Annie ladled the stew from the cooking pot into wooden bowls and broke a loaf of coarse rye bread into large chunks. Both Jake and Toby were ravenously hungry from their day working on the fen and little was said until they had finished eating.

After they had eaten the meal and washed it down with a mug of small beer, Annie counted out the money the kedger had paid her for the catch and handed half to Jake. "That's a goodly amount. With what you've brought home today we will do even better next time the kedger calls."

Jake put the coins into his pocket.

As Toby had a new burst of energy from his meal and had gone out to the yard to practise his stilt walking, Annie took the opportunity to thank Jake again for taking her son with him. "That was good of you. Did he behave?"

"Yes. He was fine. " Jake assured her.

Toby came back into the hut just as this was said. "Does that mean I can help you every day?"

"Maybe not every day. Depends what I'm doing, but some days, I'm sure. Now I must get home and get my fire lit before I settle down for the night."

Annie was pleased with this reaction. "Good. It's time he learned how to fend for himself."

Suddenly their conversation was interrupted by a loud moan from Charlie Owen, lying on his bed. "Beer" He called out. "More beer"

Annie checked the beer mug she had left by his side "Almost empty!" She sighed. "Toby." She called her son into the hut. "Take the bucket to old ma Kettle's brew house and get your grandpa some opium beer." She handed the lad a coin to pay for it.

As Toby left the hut and limped up the road past the church, towards the brew house, Annie and Jake stepped out into the fading evening light and watched the sun sinking over the marshes. Bats flitted over the hut in the half light, feeding on the clouds of insects that hovered above the thatch.

Jake lingered to talk to the girl. They watched the boy slowly vanish into the gathering dusk. "He's really been a good lad today. Very helpful."

Annie smiled her thanks. "I know he's not the fastest. With his club foot that's to be expected, but he has to learn to feed himself and make a living as he gets older."

Jake nodded silently. He was wondering how the boy came to be a cripple. He voiced the question aloud.

"How come he has that twisted foot? Did he have an accident, Annie?"

She shook her head. "No. He was born like it. It was a difficult birth. I was a young 'un; only thirteen at the time."

Jake had worked out that much for himself, knowing their present ages. "Must have been difficult for you."

"Awful." She confided. "Mum had died only a year before and dad had taken to drink. I became pregnant by accident." She looked away and hesitated. "I was raped." She whispered the confession as if she was ashamed of it.

"Raped!" Jake was incredulous. "Here in Cubbit?"

She nodded.

"Who was it, Annie?"

"I don't know." She answered in a low voice, turning her face away from him.

Jake had heard rumours in the village that Toby's father was a Cubbit boy who was a crippled simpleton. The locals were sure of the criminal's identity when Toby was born crippled because the suspect also had a club foot. He looked searchingly at his new friend. "I was told that you were attacked by the village idiot."

Annie shook her head and wouldn't meet his enquiring gaze. "It was dark. I had gone to fetch my father from the brew house when I was set upon from behind. I didn't see my attacker. He pulled my skirts over my head. I was found by Molly Kettle and some men at the brew house. They caught the cripple lad who happened to be out and about that night. They were suspicious at the time but when Toby was born with a club foot they were certain they knew who'd done it. 'Just like his father, crippled' that's what they said. They hounded the idiot boy and his mother until they left the village. I'm sure he didn't do it, but no one would listen to me."

Jake reached out and put his arm around her and tried to comfort her. "It doesn't matter anyway, Annie. Toby is far from stupid. The lad has a good head on him. He'll be alright. You mark my words." He patted her on the shoulder and apologised. "I'm sorry I asked, Annie. I had no business bringing up such matters. Forgive me. I don't know why I raised it." But in his own mind he knew full well why he needed to know what had happened. He was growing fond of the girl and wanted reassurance for himself.

She sighed. "I knew you'd want to know sooner or later. Better you hear the truth from me than the village gossips."

They fell into a companionable silence as the last rays of the sun spread a red glow over the western sky. The evening breeze got up and cooled the air, rustling the loose thatch on the hut roof.

"I'll have to get that loose thatch replaced before next winter sets in." Annie said. "That's something else Toby must learn to do." As she spoke her son loomed into view through the gathering dusk, the leather bucket of beer in his hand.

"There's a crowd of men at the church." Toby told them.

"What's going on at this time of day?" Jake asked.

"Don't know, but most of the slodgers are there and they seem very interested in a notice pinned to the church door." Toby went into the hut and placed the bucket of beer next to his grandfather's bed.

Jake stroked his chin and looked very thoughtful. "If the other men are interested I'd better go down there myself and see what's up." He said his farewell to Annie then headed to the church.

At Cubbit church Jake found most of the crowd had dispersed but a couple of local men were still there, looking closely at a handwritten notice nailed to the old oak door. He eased his way between them and started to read the notice.

"Can thee read it?" One old man asked.

"Aye." Jake continued to read the notice to himself.

"Can thee read it out loud then?" The other man suggested.

Jake, who had learned to read while he was in the army, looked at the two old fenmen and realised they weren't able to read and understand the message on the door.

"Right." He said. "It's a notice from some man called Thomas Lovell. He's asking for men to volunteer for work, digging drains and building banks on the Deeping fen. Seems they want to drain the fen and turn it into good farmland. Anyone interested needs to sign up with his agent at the White Hart Inn at Spalding, next week on market day."

"Seems like regular work. I, for one, could do with the money. What about thee lad?" The man turned to ask Jake.

"Who me? I don't think so. I've had my share of digging trenches and raising earth banks in the army. I think I'll continue working the marshes for the time being."

Jake left the men animatedly discussing the offer and walked slowly back to his hut, turning over the news in his mind and considering the implications. If the fens were drained and turned into farmland what would become of the fish and the fowl? What would happen to the ordinary working folk who relied on the bounty the fens provided to feed their families? There would be no fishing, no wildfowling, no willow grown and no turf cut for fuel. He suspected the local working folk wouldn't get any of the newly drained land; that would go to the King and the gentry. The local men would become labourers minding the sheep and cattle and ploughing the fields. That life did not appeal at all to a free spirit like himself. He didn't return to Annie's home but went straight to his own hut to consider the disturbing news.

Over the next few days little else was discussed in Cubbit. The news of impending work on the drainage gangs split the village. Jake, who occasionally called at Ma Kettles for a flagon of small beer after a hard day's trapping and fishing on the marshes, sat in the corner of her parlour and listened to the heated discussion taking place around him.

"Stands to reason I'll go and help." Bert Ward explained. "They might need an overseer and I am the fen reeve." Several of the other men glanced at him over their beers. They doubted his ability to be an overseer but they wouldn't argue with him.

"I don't agree with it." One of the oldest slodgers said. "My father and his father before him worked the fens around here and what was good enough for them is good enough for me."

"Well, maybe you can work the fens after the drainage works done." Bert suggested.

"No. Not possible." Jake interrupted and the room fell silent. The newcomer was regarded with some respect as he had travelled with the army and seen the world and they knew he could read and write. Jake continued. "After the marshes are drained, the land will be used for crops, as well as for feeding sheep and for fattening cattle. There will be no winter flooding, no fishing except a bit in the river. There will be no wildfowling because the geese and ducks will not come here any more. There will be no more cutting of turf for your fires or reeds for your thatch because there'll be no fen left."

Bert stood up and faced the young man. "What about the new jobs and the increased value of the land? That'll bring prosperity to the area. Parson Somerscal was telling me only yesterday how much he agreed with it."

"Aye, our parson would. He's a curate at Spalding church. He's in with his masters, the gentry. It's no opportunity for the likes of us." Jake shook his head. "The King, Thomas Lovell and other rich men will own the land and we will be labourers working for them. I for one, prefer to work for myself, fishing and trapping on the marshes."

"Well, there's little you can do about it so get used to the idea. It will happen whether you like it or not. Better to get what we can from it by working for Lovell." Bert spat the words out and turned his back on Jake.

Jake left Molly Kettle's brewhouse as soon as he had drained his flagon. Behind him he left a heated argument. The sounds of strident voices followed him out into the night as the men argued about the coming drainage of the fens.

Chapter Eleven

A few days after the argument in the beer house, Jake paid a visit to Spalding to pick up the saltpetre fuse that Johnny Acres had promised him. He also needed more cheese and fresh bread, which he knew he could buy in the market. He walked the three miles early that morning and was surprised to find the market place at Spalding bustling with people.

The market stalls were always set on the cobbled area in front of the White Hart inn. It was here Thomas Lovell had set his table, right outside the White Hart, to recruit able bodied men to work on draining the Deeping fen. Lovell himself sat at the head of the table, a glass in his hand and a decanter of red wine beside him. He was closely watching the proceedings as his overseer interviewed the applicants and got them to sign up for the work.

"We intend to make a start embanking the river and cutting new drains as soon as the marsh is dry enough. Hopefully that should be by mid April." Lovell told the men. "We're recruiting here, at Deeping and at Stamford because we need a large workforce to do the job over the summer while the fens are dry. If we can muster a hundred men to do the job, the marshes will be drained and they will stay dry over the winter."

The overseer explained the hours and the pay. "We are paying a good wage. One shilling a day if you bring your own victuals. Six pence a day with meat and drink provided." He promised them a full summer's work and all the hours they could muster. The Cubbit men arrived in a group with Bert Ward as their self-appointed leader.

Opinion in the village was split over the expected changes. Jake knew his way of life would have to change completely and he had no intention of staying in the area to see it happen.

Jake stood in the market and watched the proceedings. He recognised Thomas Lovell as the man he had seen near Cubbit church the day the notice was pinned to the door. It seemed the drainage of the fens was to become a reality at last. It had been talked about for years, even in the old Queen's day men had talked about it, but he never dreamed it would actually happen in his lifetime. As Jake watched his neighbours lining up to be taken on for the drainage work, Bert Ward spotted him and walked over to speak with him. "You changed your mind then. You've seen the sense in working to drain the fen?"

"No. No way." Jake shook his head emphatically.

Bert grunted his disapproval, turned abruptly on his heels, made for the recruiting table and introduced himself to the overseer. "I'm Bert Ward, the fen reeve for Cubbit. My men are used to the fens and don't mind hard work."

The overseer looked the volunteers over and saw there were eighteen of them, all able bodied and fit. "Is this all the Cubbit men?"

Bert didn't answer but one of the older men spoke up. "No sir. 'bout half I'd say."

"What about the rest of them? Aren't they interested?"

The man just shrugged his shoulders.

"Well, if they aren't going to help let's hope they aren't going to hinder the work." Lovell observed, from his seat at the end of the table.

Jake stood and watched his neighbours sign up for the drainage work.   The men willingly put their marks to the agreement then made for the nearest tavern to celebrate. He recognised most of them from the village and wasn't surprised at who had decided to join Lovell's enterprise. What did surprise him a little was the number of Cubbit men who hadn't turned up that morning. Obviously, feelings against the fen drainage ran deeper than he had anticipated. Maybe his own views, openly expressed at Molly Kettle's brewhouse, had influenced some of them. Maybe that was why Bert Ward was antagonistic towards him. He moved away from the White Hart and bought his provisions in the market before he made for Acre's workshop.

Johnny Acres had the saltpetre fuse ready for him. Jake paid for the fuse and was about to leave when he had a sudden idea. "Will you sell me some saltpetre crystals in case I run out of ready made fuse. I reckon I might use quite a bit of it, waiting in hiding in the fen with the gun at the ready." The matchlock gun required the fuse to be kept lit, ready and waiting to fire the black powder charge at the opportune moment. That waiting could stretch to some time, and it was no use spotting the quarry then striking a flint to light the fuse; that would take too long and frighten the wildfowl away with the noise and the sudden movement.

"Aye. I can spare an ounce or two. Do you know how to use it?"

"I've spent the past few years serving in Ireland under Robert Devereux. I'm no stranger to matchlocks. I'll dissolve it in water and soak my own rope in it."

Johnny weighed out the saltpetre and wrapped it in a twist of paper. He handed it over with a warning. "Keep it dry or it turns to water with the moisture in the air."

Jake thanked him and walked back into town to buy his other provisions. By the time he arrived at the market and the White Hart, the Cubbit men had all departed for the local inns or for home.

Jake walked the short distance back to Cubbit at a slow pace, not wishing to catch up with Bert Ward and his gang.

With Jake away in Spalding and time on his hands, Toby decided to try his hand at bird trapping for himself. He took a net and rope and walked onto the marsh towards the river. Reluctant to manage the punt by himself, he decided to walk along the river bank and set his net in one of the reed beds, where herons and bitterns lurked.

Toby placed his trap as Jake had shown him, but being a young lad and on his own with no adult to restrain him, he failed to keep absolutely still and quiet. Patience was not one of Toby's strong points but after several fruitless hours of waiting, the lad was fast losing interest. Eventually, after five separate attempts to catch something, Toby did catch a bird. A single small bird became trapped in the mesh of his net. He leapt on the prize with glee. At last he had something to prove he could use a net to trap birds. Toby held the tiny bird gently in his hand to avoid crushing it. Laid on its back in the boys hand, the bird stopped struggling and panted through its open beak.

"Ah! A linnet!" Toby recognised the songbird from its reddish feathering. "You little beauty. You can come home with me and sing for my mother." Pleased with his catch the boy placed the bird in a small sack, gathered up his net and limped across the marsh to his home.

"Where have you been?" Annie looked sternly at her son when he eventually arrived home. "I needed you to go to Ma Kettle's for your grandpa."

Toby shrugged his shoulder and smiled.

Annie, aware that he seemed in an exceptionally good mood, eyed him up and down. "Well? What have you been up to? Why are you so pleased with yourself?"

"I've been netting on the fen."

"Ah! And did you catch anything?"

Toby put his hand into the bag and drew out the tiny Linnet he had trapped. "A songbird for you. It will keep you company and cheer you up when I'm out with Jake."

Annie looked at the small feathered bundle and softened her voice. "Poor little creature." She said. "What am I supposed to do with a wild bird? It's too small to eat and it should be free."

Toby shook his head . "I caught it especially for you. You can make a willow cage for it. I've seen them in cages and they sing beautifully."

Annie was in two minds what to do. She felt the bird should be free to lead its own life but she knew that would upset Toby, who had brought it especially for her. Finally she said. "Keep it safe and I will weave a cage for it after we've eaten. We can hang it near the door where your grandpa and I can hear it singing. Now you must go to the beer house for some opium beer for your grandpa."

Toby was thrilled with his catch and his mother's attitude. He whistled happily as he made his way to Ma Kettle's brewhouse with his jug.

Chapter Twelve

Early in the summer, work started on raising earth banks along the river Welland and on digging new dykes and clearing existing ones that were clogged with vegetation and silt. The gang of Cubbit men set out at first light each morning to dig the fen and build the new banks to contain the river water. Further over the marshes, across the river Welland, similar gangs of workmen from the Deepings and as far as Stamford were working on their parts of the ambitious drainage scheme.

Jake moored his boat some way from the earthworks and paddled upriver towards the Deepings to avoid any contact with the gangs of workers. So far the disturbance to the fens was minimal and made no difference to the fishing and wildfowling but he could see there would soon be a clash of interests.

One evening as Jake walked back across the fen towards Cubbit, his catch strung along a pole over his shoulder, he noticed a group of workmen standing near the church. As he drew nearer he recognised them all as members of Bert Ward's gang of labourers. They seemed to be disturbed and talking animatedly to each other for he could hear the sound of raised voices. Jake changed direction and walked further over the fen towards his own hut to avoid any contact with them. He knew some of them, Bert Ward in particular, still held a grudge against him for arguing against the drainage scheme.

At Annie's hut he unloaded the day's catch and stopped to take a rest. He asked. "What's going on at the church, Annie?"

"I don't know. I saw them carrying a large sack between them but I don't know what was in it. Maybe Toby will know more when he gets back here. He's gone to Ma Kettles for dad's brew. Come in and have a drink and wait for him."

Jake was glad of a rest. He sat on the reed floor propped up against the hut wall and drank a mug of small beer while he chatted idly to Annie.

When Toby came in he was full of excitement. "They've brought a dead body off the fen, Mum." He blurted out as soon as he was though the doorway.

Jake got up. "A body? Has someone had an accident on the drainage gang?"

"No. They reckon its been buried near the river for years."

Annie joined in the exchange. "Do they think they know who it is?"

Toby put the beer down beside his grandpa's bed. "They say it's the body of a man. He could have got into the quicksands years ago. But it's not just a skeleton it's a whole body with skin and hair and clothes.. "

"Must be a recent death." Annie suggested

Jake shook his head. "The boggy conditions on the marshes tend to preserve bodies. When I was a lad living here in Cubbit, they found a horseman buried under the road when a freak tide broke the bank down. They reckoned he'd been drowned ages before but he looked as if he'd only been there a short time."

"Who could it be and how would he have died?" Annie asked.

Jake shook his head. He knew there were patches of quicksand on the fen, especially in the winter months when the tides flooded the whole area. The locals understood these hazards. Perhaps it was a stranger trying to cross the marshes.

By next morning the magistrate at Spalding had been told of the find and a constable was sent out to Cubbit to investigate the body. Jake went up the river to check his traps, this time taking Toby with him.

By mid afternoon the locals were stunned by the news from the constable investigation. Rumour spread through the village that the dead man had been murdered. The investigator had found the skull broken, apparently fractured by a heavy blow to the head. The unexplained death had suddenly become a murder investigation. By evening when Jake and Toby returned home, the village was in an uproar. The body had been identified as that of Peter Small, the simpleton who had left the village under a cloud some ten years earlier!

The magistrate's representative had set up an enquiry in the church to question people about the body and several locals had come forward and identified the boy's tattered blue coat. The state of preservation of the body, which still had traces of red hair clinging to the head and a definite club foot, left no doubt that this was indeed Peter Small. Now the investigation would turn to the time the boy and his mother left the village and the events leading up to their departure.

Ma Kettle, being at the ale house in the centre of the village, heard all the village tittle tattle before most of her neighbours. She had been one of the witnesses called to identify the body and realised how this news might affect Annie Owen. She walked down to the Owen's hut to tell them what was being said.

Annie was busy weaving eel traps when Ma Kettle arrived. Her father was fast asleep on his bed, drugged by the opium beer. She was surprised to see the old woman away from the brewhouse and rose to greet her. "Is something wrong Ma? You don't often come this far from your home."

The old woman told Annie all she had heard about the body found in the fen. As she left the stunned girl she turned and warned her. "They may want to see you, Annie, about the reason Peter left the village all those years ago."

Annie gasped and clutched her hand to her breast. She thought all of that was in the past and best forgotten. She was devastated by this news. Her rape and Toby's birth would become the subject of village gossip once again and she had never discussed those matters with her son.

Later in the afternoon, as soon as Toby and Jake returned from fishing, she turned to Jake for support. She started to blurt out what had happened but broke down in tears.

Jake, seeing her distress, put his arm around her shoulders. "What's the problem, Annie? Who is this Peter Small?"

"That's the crippled lad they blamed for my rape."

"I thought you said he and his mother had been driven out of the village and had taken to the roads?"

"That's what we were told. One morning the locals found their hut was burned to the ground and they had left the village."

Jake scratched his head, deep in thought. A body buried in the fen made him think of foul play. If the boy and his mother had walked away from the village, being local they would have taken the main road and not a dangerous path across the fen. This was a mystery that would take some explaining. He voiced his fears to his companion. "Could be we have a murder in the area."

Annie dried her eyes and nodded vigorously. "They are saying the skull was bashed in and murder is suspected."

Jake shook his head then asked abruptly. "What about his mother? Didn't you say the boy and his mother left the village together?"

"As far as I know they did. That's what everyone assumed."

"It strikes me there could be another body out there in the fen. But knowing the way the mud banks shift it could be years before it comes to light, if it ever does."

Once Jake had left and walked to his own hut, Annie took Toby to one side and tried to explain to him what had happened to her all those years ago; how he came to be born and how the village blamed the dead man for his birth. The boy took all of this news in silence and seemed stunned by it. He stood transfixed, his head bowed. Annie quickly changed the subject. She put her arms around him to hug him closer to her and asked "Would you like some soup?"

Toby shook his head, pushed her away and hobbled out of the hut along the road towards the church. The shock of hearing about his own beginnings had shaken him to the core. His mother could only stand at the doorway and watch him go. She was devastated by the events of that day and even more worried about her son. In a desperate cry for help she turned and ran to Jake's hut and begged him to follow her boy to help him come to terms with the awful news.

Toby had walked to the church before Jake caught up with him. The boy tried to get in to see Peter Small's body but found the door was locked. He was banging on the oak door with his fists when Jake finally joined him.

"What are you hoping to do, Toby?" Jake asked

"I don't know...I just wanted to see this body...he could be my father..."

"No he isn't. Your mother was adamant about that. She couldn't identify her assailant but she knew it wasn't Peter Small."

"How do you know this? You didn't live here at the time."

"No, but your mother did explain it all to me some time ago."

"She told you but she hadn't bothered to tell me! I should have guessed there was some secret about my birth. Some of the local kids I grew up with, have hinted as much."

"Your mother didn't tell you because she was shielding you from it. Anyway, what difference does it make now? You have a happy home and you are learning to make a living on the fens with me.

Nothing has changed, Toby. Your mother still loves you. Your grandpa loves you. I respect you for the hard work you do. Nothing has changed."

Toby burst into tears and sat down on one of the weathered gravestones. Jake sat beside him. After a few minutes when the boy's sobs had subsided a little, Jake put his arm around his shoulders.

"Think of your mum, Toby. She's carried this problem all her young life but she has brought you up and she has stood by and nursed your grandpa as well as earning a meagre living making the traps and nets. You are growing into a young man and can now take your place helping the family to survive."

Toby dried his eyes and sadly shook his head. "I wish she'd told me before. This has been a shock."

Jake pushed the lad to his feet. "Come on home. Your mother's fretting about you and you haven't eaten yet after a busy day fishing. Better keep your strength up for tomorrow's work."

Chapter Thirteen.

The following day, some time after Jake and Toby had set out to fish the river, the Spalding constable accompanied by Thomas Lovell himself, galloped into Cubbit. The church was commandeered to hold an enquiry into the suspicious death.

Lovell had accompanied his overseer to the dig where the body had come to light but nothing more was unearthed. There was no sign of another body even though the boy and his mother left the village on the same night, nor was there any clue how Peter Small's body came to be there.

The constable from Spalding, John Brewer, wasted no time in calling witnesses to testify at the hearing. The men who had discovered the body were questioned first, then other members of the community who were living in the village when the boy and his mother left the area. Molly Kettle was one of these later witnesses.

The constable asked the questions while a clerk noted down the answers.

"Molly Kettle. You keep the brewhouse here?"

"Yes sir. Have done for many years."

"I understand you knew the dead man and his mother."

"Yes sir. Peter and Mrs Small were occasionally customers of mine for the opium beer to treat the winter ague. They had lived in the village for years."

"What do you know about them leaving the village?"

Ma Kettle wet her lips nervously and looked around the crowded church. Bert Ward and his friends were hanging on her very word.

"There was a rumour that the lad raped a local girl, Sir. He was shunned for this. I think that's why he and his ma left the area."

The constable looked at her in silence for some time then he said. "This could prove to be a murder case. Rape would be a good enough reason for some people to murder a man. What do you think happened?"

Molly looked down at her feet. She had witnessed the awful vengeance that Bert Ward and his mates had inflicted on Peter Small that evening in her kitchen when they had castrated him. She shuffled her feet but said nothing more.

John Brewer tried again. "Who was raped? Does the girl still live in the village? Has she a family? Maybe a father or brothers who might want revenge?"

Bert Ward cleared his throat and spoke up. "Begging your pardon, sir. I'm the village reeve and I can help here."

John Brewer turned to face the speaker. "Well, man?"

"The girl is Annie Owen she lives on the Spalding road, just up from the church. She has a young son, the result of this rape, and she has a father, but no brothers."

"Get her and her father here. I need to question them."

Bert Ward shuffled his feet nervously. "I'm sure Annie will come but her father is at death's door from the ague. He wouldn't be any use to you, Sir."

The constable rose from his chair and folded his papers. "We will adjourn for refreshment but I want this girl, Annie Owen, brought before me after we've eaten."

The locals shuffled out of the church to get their own food and drink, blinking in the bright sunlight as they spilled out into the churchyard. The clerk stopped Molly Kettle at the door and asked her where he could find Annie.

"I'll go and get her, sir." Molly promised.

After the break, Annie walked to the church accompanied by Molly to give her moral support.

John Brewer reconvened his hearing and asked Annie to stand before him. "You are Annie Owen?"

"Yes sir." Annie's voice wavered with nerves.

"I understand you were raped and many of your neighbours blamed Peter Small for the crime?"

"Yes sir... but Peter didn't do it."

"Ah! So who did rape you?"

Annie hesitated and looked at her feet. At last she spoke. "I don't know Sir. But I do know it wasn't Peter."

The constable frowned. "How can you be sure?"

"I knew Peter, Sir. The man who raped me was much bigger and had a gruffer voice."

Jon Brewer nodded. "But you didn't recognise your assailant?"

Again Annie seemed to hesitate. Finally she shook her head. "No Sir."

A murmur of disappointed voices broke out in the church. They had been hanging on her every word hoping for some new information.

"Silence." John Brewer banged on the table. "This is a serious business. We are hearing a possible murder case here." He dismissed Annie and went into a discussion with his clerk.

The rest of the constable's day was taken up with more witnesses but Annie went home.

On the suggestion of Thomas Lovell, Bert Ward and two of the drainage gang were questioned about finding the body. They hinted that someone may have disturbed the corpse while digging the trench where it was found.

"It's possible one of my men hit the skull with his shovel and caused the damage to it." Bert asserted. "It's also possible a boat may have collided with the body if it was at the bottom of the river when he first died. The Welland is always moving its course over the fens so he could have been in the bed of the river until recently."

Lovell nodded vigorous agreement. He did not want any further investigation of his drainage site to hold up the work. "It may even have been suicide," he suggested to the constable.

After she had been questioned by the constable, Annie had walked home. She passed by the patch of overgrown earth where the Small's hut had once stood and hesitated beside it. Before she moved on she stopped for a few minutes and whispered a prayer for them both.

The constable's final verdict was death by natural causes. He decided there was no case to pass to the Justice of the Peace in Spalding so there would be no full inquest. The body was finally laid to rest in a pauper's grave in the far corner of the churchyard. Bert Ward and a few of his friends put the word about that the boy and his mother had probably been murdered by footpads for their meagre belongings or they had killed themselves because of the rape allegations. Most of the locals doubted those explanations as they knew Peter and his mother were destitute and had nothing worth stealing, they had also heard Annie deny the boy was involved in her rape, but they kept their doubts to themselves.

The day after the burial Annie went onto the fen and picked some wild flowers and laid them on the newly dug grave beside a similar posy that someone else had already placed there. This surprised her a little as most of the village hadn't a good word to say about the Small family. She knew that Peter had been as much a victim of her rape as she had.

She stood in silence and said a prayer for his soul then turned and walked to the far side of the churchyard where her own mother, Gwendoline Owen, had been buried some years before. Once again there was no stone to mark her mother's resting place but the position of that unmarked grave was etched on Annie's memory. She bent down and placed a posy of wild flowers on her mother's grave and whispered another prayer.

As Annie left the churchyard and closed the gate she was greeted by Molly Kettle, who was walking her dog.

"Been to your mam's grave again have you, love?"

Annie nodded and smiled at the old woman.

"I've seen you here week in and week out since Gwen died, whatever the weather. You're a good girl, Annie, and you have grown to look exactly like your mother. When I glanced into the churchyard as I walked the dog just now, I took a second look at you standing at the grave. You reminded me so much of your late mother. She was very pretty. Just like you."

Annie blushed at this compliment and quickly changed the subject "I've just put a bunch of flowers on Peter Small's grave. He didn't deserve to die like that."

Molly nodded agreement. "I never did believe the things they were saying about the lad. He was simple enough but that didn't make him a criminal."

When she returned home Annie stood outside her door listening to the caged bird that Toby had trapped. The tiny Linnet was singing its heart out answering the calls of the wild birds it could hear on the fen. On impulse she opened the door of the willow cage and let the little bird fly out. She watched it fly across the marsh to a reed bed and join a flock of other Linnets. She knew she would have to make some excuse to Toby when he returned from fishing but she felt in her heart the tiny wild bird deserved to live its life flying free. She knew that that freedom was what she dearly wished for herself. Life was too short to spend it shut in a cage.

Chapter Fourteen

Each day Jake went further on the river, avoiding the gangs of workmen, to catch the fish and eels, and to trap the wildfowl that earned him his living. Some days he took Toby with him. As the drainage work progressed there were signs that the marshy areas were beginning to dry out. Jake knew that the coming winter, when the fen would normally return to being flooded, would be a turning point in the drainage work. Lovell was pushing the work on at a great rate to ensure the river banks and the newly cut drains would keep the fen free of standing water; that way the land would dry out and eventually be fit to be put under the plough. When that day came, Jake knew the fens and his way of life as a slodger would be finished. It was a sobering thought that he and hundreds of other fen men would have to find other ways to earn a living. He knew in his heart that he would have to leave his new home and move on again.

The changes to the area, which Jake had noticed, were not wasted on the other slodgers. They grumbled amongst themselves. A restless feeling spread across the fens. The Cubbit men discussed the situation quietly to themselves, taking care not to antagonise Bert Ward and the men who had taken Lovell's money and were spoiling the fishing and trapping.

"How am I going to feed a growing family?" One father asked his mate in the brewhouse.

"Search me. I'm at a loss. My father and his father before him worked the marshes. I don't know owt else. Stands to reason I can't suddenly learn farm work. I'm too old for it."

One of Lovells's workmen who happened to be in Molly Kettle's that night answered their questions. "There'll be lots of land. Acres and acres of it. You'll be able to farm and to do farm labouring. It'll pay better and be dryer work. You mark my words."

This promise of money and work to come seemed to placate most of the slodgers, but Jake who had seen more of the world, had his doubts.

One morning, matters came to a head. A group of men rode into Cubbit and tethered their horses near the church. They set to with chains and measures marking out the land that would soon be drained for ever. As they measured the land they hammered wooden stakes into the fen, dividing it up into parcels of land. Several of the local men knew the Spalding surveyors and went to speak with them.

"What's thee about then?"

"Marking out the land that Thomas Lovell will hold when it's completely drained. By next year he'll be running store cattle on this fen all year round and in a few years, when the salt has leached from the soil, he'll be growing wheat, barley, rye and beans on it."

Jake happened to be passing the group who were discussing the surveying. He stopped to listen, then asked. "Where's my patch of land? I need somewhere to grow my crops to compensate me for the loss of my living off the fen."

The surveyor laughed out loud. "Your land, lad? Depends if you can afford to buy it. Lovell has been granted over a ten thousand acres by my reckoning, to recompense him for his work and his investment. The rest goes to the King. Gentry folk, like Sir John Gamlyn and Lord Burleigh will buy acres of it from the King. You'll have to buy it too. Nobody's going to give it away."

The surveyors got on with the task of measuring and dividing the land leaving the slodgers talking and arguing amongst themselves. Finally one of the men, hotter headed than the rest, declared he wouldn't tolerate the theft of their fen.

"What can ye do about it, Tom?" Another asked

"I have a cousin in the Deepings. He hasn't joined the drainage gangs either. We'll see what we can do about it." He turned to his companions. "How about it? Are you with me for a bit of dyke and bank destruction?"

The positive replies left Jake in no doubt the mood was turning angry. He walked away from the group and kept his own counsel. He was young and unfettered by family responsibilities, and wiser in the ways of the world. His army service had taught him to be self-sufficient. If the living on the fens failed he would move and try something else. Leaving the plotters behind, Jake walked across the fen to the river where he had left his boat. He had every intention of checking his eel traps and his deadlines for fish, but the boat was nowhere to be found.

As the work of the gangs drew nearer to the part of the river where Jake liked to moor his punt, he had moved it further inland towards Crowland to be well away from them. He knew he had tethered the craft securely when he had last used it. It was second nature to him to drag the boat clear of the water and rope it down. Someone must have untied the boat and pushed it into the river. As he had no way of knowing what time the theft had occurred and which way the river was flowing at the time, he had the problem of guessing which way the boat had gone. He walked up and down the muddy bank of the Welland and tried to read the marks left on the mud flats to work out what had happened.

After some careful consideration, Jake decided the boat was pushed onto the outgoing tide and would have drifted along the river towards Spalding and the sea. He wasn't sure how long the punt had been free of its moorings as he hadn't fished for the two previous days. There was nothing for it but to walk the river bank into Spalding, looking for signs of his boat as he went.

Jake's path took him through the area where the gangs were working on the drainage scheme. He tried to avoid eye contact with the Cubbit men that he knew, but Bert Ward made it his business to shout to him.

"After a job then?"

Jake shook his head.

The reeve stopped his work and pushed his hands onto his hips. "You look as if you've lost something, lad."

Jake tried to ignore the taunts.

"Wouldn't be that boat we saw floating past two days ago. Would it?"

Jake quickened his pace and distanced himself from the gang. He was suspicious of Ward and his comments and even suspected the man of being involved in the theft of his boat but he kept his thoughts to himself. He jogged along the river bank until he was well out of sight of the workers then slowed his pace to a fast walk.

Jake walked all the way into Spalding and still had no sight of his lost boat. Finally he got to the docks in the centre of town and sat down at the dockside to check the scores of small boats moored there. It took him some time to check out every boat but happily he spotted his lost punt tied at a private jetty on the far side of the river. He walked over the old stone bridge to the town side of the river to retrieve his property.

"You looking for someone, mate?" A dock worker challenged Jake as he walked down the private pathway to the wooden jetty where his boat was moored.

"That's my punt." Jake pointed to his boat. "It came loose from its moorings at Cubbit and was washed down here."

"Ah! The punt. I suppose you can prove you're the owner. I've been asking about the docks since I hooked it in and moored it to our jetty. No one seems to be able to identify it."

"Check in the bottom of it." Jake said. "There's a hand made willow oar, a willow eel trap and some nets in there."

"Alright my friend. The boat's yours. Tie it up more securely next time you leave it on the river."

Jake was about to explain he had left it high and dry on the bank and someone had pushed it into the tide but he thought better of it. The important thing was he had Charlie's boat back again. Now he had to wait for the incoming tide to propel him and the boat back to the Cubbit fen or he must paddle the whole way back against the outgoing currents. He turned to the dock worker and thanked him for looking after the craft. "I'll have to wait for the incoming tide before I paddle the boat back upstream. Can I buy you a flagon of beer for your troubles.?"

"Very civil of you." The man accompanied Jake to the dockside tavern where they enjoyed a beer or two together.

By the time the tide was running well inland the light was beginning to fade. Jake set out to paddle the boat in the failing light the few miles to the fen. He let the punt ride the tide only occasionally using his paddle to correct its course. The muddy water bubbled and swirled about him making strange noises in the half light. Once he was clear of the town the river ran slower, getting sluggish as it entered the fen. Water birds like Heron and Bittern cried out and rose in the half light as he approached them. Coots and Water Hens clucked quietly as they took their last feed before sleeping.

A Fox crested the bank on one side and stood watching him as he paddle by, its bushy tail trailing in the mud as it quartered the fen looking for some unwary water bird.

Jake was in no hurry to get back to Cubbit. He hoped the gang of drainage workers was long gone so that he could return the boat upstream and find a good hiding place for it unseen. As he passed the area where he had seen Bert Ward that morning he was pleased to see work had finished for the day. The new, high, mud banks that the workmen were building towered over the river cutting out his views of the fen beyond them.

By the time the sun had sunk over the Crowland fen and the moon had risen over the silvered water, Jake was some way past the spot where he usually moored the boat. He continued for another mile to a place where he thought he could hide it securely. The drainage engineers had not started on that stretch of the river and there was a dense reed bed near the water's edge. In the moonlight he pulled the boat onto the bank and hid it completely in the reeds. He knew he would eventually have to move it again when the drainage gangs moved upriver to that area, but for the time being he felt it was safe there.

The new mooring for the punt was much further from his home in Cubbit so he set out to walk across the fen to the Crowland road. Here he mounted the embankment and walked along the dirt track to Cubbit, passing the church and Annie's cottage on his way home.

Once home Jake lit a fire and prepared his supper. He was laying back on his bed on the floor, eating a simple meal of bread and cheese when he became aware of a bump pressing into his back. That obstruction had not been there before. He always smoothed his bed of reeds and grasses when he got up in the morning. He realised something was not quite right!

Jake finished his meal then poked his fire to get a dancing flame and more light. He felt under the layers of reeds and grasses to understand what the lump was in his bed. Unable to work out what had happened, Jake pulled his bedding up from the floor to reveal a newly disturbed heap of soil. Something or someone had been digging in his hut!

"The gun!" Jake exclaimed as one possible reason for the disturbance leapt into his mind. Quickly he checked the hiding place for his matchlock only to find it had gone! While he had been occupied finding the punt and bringing it back to Cubbit someone had searched his hut and stolen the firearm. A further search revealed that the thief had not only taken the gun, the black powder, shot and fuse, which he had hidden, were stolen as well. Whoever had the gun had the means to use it.

As he lay on his bed drinking a mug of small beer, Jake thought over the day's events. Someone or some persons had taken the trouble to steal his boat and his matchlock gun. There were very few people in the area who knew of the gun's existence. There was the blacksmith who had repaired the serpentine for him and Johnny Acres who had sold him the fuse and black powder. There was Toby, but he dismissed the boy from his list immediately. Then he suddenly remembered Bert Ward asking about the firearm at the blacksmith's shop. That man was cropping up far too often in his life.

Jake only wanted a quiet existence. After his army experience and getting wounded, he had returned home to the fens hoping to find peace and spend his days fishing and trapping. Now someone seemed hell bent on spoiling those hopes.

"They'll find me far from quiet and peaceful when I find out who is behind this trouble." Jake muttered to the empty hut. Next morning he was determined to find out what had happened.

Chapter Fifteen.

Next morning Jake rose early and reported the theft of his matchlock gun to Bert Ward. As reeve, Bert was the only figure of any authority in the village. Bert took the news in silence.

"I'll report it in Spalding as well." Jake informed him. "That's the nearest place with magistrates. They may come across my firearm".

"Could be a passing thief. Could be miles away by now. Pity you didn't hide it better." Those were Bert's parting comments.

Jake walked back to his hut and passed the time of day with Annie as she stood in her doorway.

"You're about early." She said.

"Had to be. Needed to report a theft to the reeve."

"Theft?" Annie was puzzled; what had Jake got worth stealing?

"You remember that old matchlock gun from my army days. It's gone. Taken while I was returning your boat to the fen."

Annie shook her head in disbelief. She believed that no one in the village had need to lock their doors. They were all poor and needy but they wouldn't steal from each other. Cubbit folk were more likely to give you a crust then take one from you. Finally she asked. "Any idea who may have taken it?"

"No. To be honest I have no idea, but I must go into Spalding and report it, in case someone gets shot with it. If it turns up at the scene of a crime it has my initials on it."

Annie bid him a good journey then turned indoors to get breakfast and start on her chores.

By the time Jake arrived in Spalding the place was busy. The docks were alive with craft being loaded and unloaded. Barrels of wine and bolts of woollen cloth were being unloaded while sheep fleeces and tanned cow skins were being hauled aboard the outgoing merchant ships. Dockers worked stripped to the waist, sweating from their labours. Spalding enjoyed a busy exchange with the near continent and with the ports on England's eastern seaboard such as Boston, Lynn and even London.

At the blacksmiths, Jake asked the smith to look out for his gun. The man knew the weapon as he had repaired it. "Rest assured I'll know that gun again if I set eyes on it, lad."

Jake next asked Johnny Acres to keep an eye out for anything unusual in the demand for fuses and black powder, then he walked to the town centre and reported the theft to the clerk of the magistrates and the town constable. Satisfied he could do no more, he returned to Cubbit where he called on Annie to explain what had happened.

Finding the girl on her own with her father, Jake asked "Where's Toby?"

"He's up at the churchyard. There's some sort of meeting about the drainage work on the fen."

"Recruiting more diggers, are they?"

"No. It's the slodgers who don't agree with the scheme. They are protesting about it."

Jake nodded ; he had already heard the rumblings of dissent.

"I'm not happy Toby is getting involved." Annie said. "He's only a young lad and easily led."

"I'll take a walk up there, if you like. I need to keep abreast of what's happening for my own peace of mind."

"Would you? Thanks Jake. I worry about my son."

As Jake walked up to the church, he could hear raised voices well before he reached the crowd of men.

"Who's with me then?" Thomas Skinner, the man who Jake had heard loudly complaining the previous day, was rallying support. "We'll tear down those banks and stop them thieving our land and our livings."

Jake stood on the edge of the meeting and looked for Toby. The boy was small and easily lost in a crowd but finally Jake spotted him near the church doorway. Sidling through the crowd, Jake made his way to Toby's side.

"Ah! Jake." Toby beamed when he saw his friend. "Have you come to help stop the drainage scheme?"

Jake shook his head. "No. And if you have any sense you'll not get involved. You could get hurt and you could end up in Spalding gaol. Your mother has sent me to bring you home. Come on."

Reluctantly Toby followed Jake from the churchyard to his home. "It's not right. They are taking the fishing and trapping away from local folk. What will my mother and I do then to earn a living?"

Jake couldn't answer that question. He just shook his head and remained tight lipped and silent.

When they arrived at Toby's home his mother was waiting at the door for him. She thanked Jake for bringing her son home then asked him to come inside.

"What's going to happen?" She asked a deep frown on her face.

"I honestly don't know, Annie. But if they do attack the drainage work there will be fights and violence. Some one is sure to be hurt and the law will put some in gaol. Keep Toby away from them if you can. He's only a young lad and too small for fighting with grown men."

"And you?"

"I've seen enough fighting and killing in Ireland to last me my lifetime."

Annie persisted in her questions. "What if the fen is drained? What will you do then?"

"I don't know, but I will not slave on another man's land. I will have to move on if the trapping and fishing go."

The girl looked down at her feet and didn't ask any more questions.

That night the Cubbit slodgers joined with the Deeping men and attacked the drainage works. They overthrew the newly built earth banks and threw the tools into the deepest parts of the river. The water, recently contained in the narrow river channel, flooded out onto the fen once again, undoing weeks of back breaking work. Next morning when Lovell's overseer inspected the damage there was uproar. Later in the day Lovell and several of his supporters road into Cubbit intent on stopping the riots.

Jake, who had heard of the disturbance, stood at his hut door and watched the riders gallop by towards the church and the centre of the village. Thomas Lovell, easily identified by his yellow surcoat and large hat, was in the lead, followed closely by his local overseer and several men. Martin Somerscal, the curate in Spalding who served as curate at Cubbit, brought up the rear.

Jake retired into his hut and remained there, little interested in the comings and goings of the village.

The villagers who had attacked the works under the cover of darkness the previous night, melted away and did not stop to hear what Lovell and his men had to say. A notice was nailed to the church door offering a reward for information leading to the apprehension of the people who had torn down the new drainage banks. By nightfall that notice had been ripped off the oak door and had vanished.

Chapter Sixteen

A few days after the first attack on the drainage works, Jake was at Molly Kettles in the early evening, quenching his thirst after a day's fishing. When he entered the room he found three other men were already drinking there. This group were engaged in a whispered and earnest conversation, which stopped abruptly on his arrival. One of the group, Tom Skinner, a man Jake knew slightly, passed the time of day with Jake then asked him, "How about you, Jake? You can't be thrilled with this drainage business. What ya going to do when the fens are all gone?"

Jake shrugged his shoulders. "I'm a single man. I have no one but myself to please. I can move on."

"Hmm! That's not so easy for most of us. We have families in the village."

The other men agreed with Tom.

"We wondered if you were thinking of joining the wrecking gang?"

Jake shook his head. "Sorry, no. I've seen enough fighting to last me a lifetime. But I wish the wreckers well, whoever they are."

Relieved at Jake's attitude, Tom asked, "Are you sure you're not interested? You'd be a useful ally, you having army experience."

Jake shook his head emphatically.

Tom nervously licked his lips then continued. "Would you have any objection if some of the wreckers borrowed your punt? It would help them get behind the guards under the cover of darkness."

Jake shrugged his shoulders. "I wouldn't worry about things I didn't see, but bear in mind that punt belongs to Annie Owen, and it's not mine to lend."

The conversation came to an abrupt halt as Bert Ward and two of his cronies came into the room. The three men turned their backs on the newcomers and drained their mugs of beer.

Bert, aware that the room had gone quiet at his arrival, turned to the four occupants. "Don't suppose you lot know who has been breaking down the new river banks?" He eyed them suspiciously as he spoke.

The men shook their heads.

"Whoever they are, they'll get caught and the full weight of the law will be brought down on them. The King himself has an interest in draining this wetland."

Tom Skinner spoke up. "I heard they was Deeping men, coming up the river to break down the banks."

His two companions readily agreed with him. Jake said nothing.

"What about you, Jake Fowler? Have you seen or heard anything while you were fishing the fens?" Bert stared intently at the young man.

Jake shook his head and returned the stare, but still said nothing.

Bert Ward, realising he was getting nowhere, just grunted and sat down with his companions to drink his beer. Tom Skinner and his two friends quickly drained their mugs and left. Jake sat alone slowly savouring his drink then he left to go home for his evening meal.

As Jake passed Annie's hut, Tom Skinner came out of her doorway. He put his hand up to acknowledge Jake and stopped to talk with him.

"That Bert Ward gets right under my skin! He's only too pleased to take Lovell's money with no thought for the future or for his neighbours."

Jake agreed.

"Annie says I can borrow her punt as long as you agree."

Jake nodded. He'd guessed that was why Skinner had called on his neighbour. "Just leave it moored where you find it and I won't know anything about it." He watched the man walk back towards the church and the main body of the village then he turned and went to speak to Annie.

Inside the Owen's home, Charlie was snoring on his bed and Annie and Toby were sitting cross legged on the floor weaving willow wands into eel traps. As soon as Jake entered the room she rose to her feet and went to greet him. Toby grinned up at their visitor, pleased to see him.

"I see Tom Skinner called on you then."

"Yes. He wants to borrow the punt occasionally. I told him as long as you didn't need it and you agreed to it, that was alright."

"Did he tell you why he wanted it?"

Annie hesitated and didn't reply.

Jake nodded. "I see that he did... Are you alright with him using the boat to sabotage the new banks?"

Again Annie hesitated, then she blurted out. "If the fens are drained. What'll I do to live? Toby and I rely on the eel trapping and the fishing. You will leave the area, Jake; you've said as much several times. We don't want to lose you." Tears came into her eyes and ran down her pale cheeks.

Toby got up from the floor and stood at his mother's side. "Don't go, Jake. Who'd teach me to fish and hunt if you go?"

Jake was taken aback at this unexpected show of emotion. He had indeed voiced several times his intention to move on if the fens were drained and they became farmlands. Now, for the first time, he had pangs of regret at the thought of leaving Cubbit. He had not realised how intertwined his life had become with Annie Owen and her son. He gave the girl a hug and mumbled "We'll have to cross that bridge when we come to it, Annie. Maybe the wreckers will be successful and stop the drainage scheme."

"I do hope so." The girl sighed.

Jake left the Owen's hut and walked slowly to his own home, deep in thought at the recent turn of events. He had had no intention of getting involved in the fight for the fens but now his resolve wavered. He sat down and ate his evening meal musing over the conversation with Annie and Toby. Slowly he began to realise he would miss her and her son if he had to move away from the area. Jake had enjoyed no settled existence since his parents died and he'd joined the army. He had moved about England and Ireland wherever his services were needed and had put down no roots. Now he had returned to the Lincolnshire fens he felt at home again and more settled than he had ever felt before in his adult life, and he suddenly realised Annie and her son were a big part of that feeling. This drainage business was a damned nuisance and very unsettling.

After his meal Jake sat outside his hut and watched the sun sink over the marshes. Ducks and geese rose from their daytime feeding grounds and flew out towards the East, to safer roosts on the coast of the Wash. Their vee formations were etched black against the bright pink of the evening sky. Their voices rang out plaintively over the still marshes as they called to each other in the gathering dusk.

A grey Heron flew lazily across the fen towards the river. All this beauty and all this bounty will be gone, Jake mused, and all for what? All because rich landowners coveted even more farmland. His way of life and that of his forebears and his neighbours would be gone forever. The fen slodgers counted for nothing in this affair.

He threw himself onto his bed for the night but couldn't sleep as his mind was full of images of the changes to the fens. Annie's tearstained face kept coming into his mind, but still he felt reluctant to join in with the wreckers. He had experienced enough violence and bloodshed in the Irish campaign to last him a lifetime. He hesitated to help the wreckers but felt guilty that he wasn't helping them. His mind was in a turmoil but his instinct was to leave well alone. Jake drank some of his Opium beer and eventually slipped into a troubled sleep.

Some time after midnight, Jake woke up in a cold sweat. He woke up screaming at the hut wall and clutching his damaged shoulder. As the nightmare subsided he realised he had relived for the hundredth time, the battle in Ireland when he was shot. He lay in the darkness breathing deeply and cursing the constantly recurring nightmares. After a few minutes he got up from his bed and stepped outside his hut door into the night. Leaning his back against the door he stared out over the fen at the stars twinkling above him and listened to the sounds of the night all about him while his nightmare faded and he returned to normal.

The peace and quite he had hoped to find in the fens was being shattered by the attempts to drain the whole area. He could understand the fen men fighting against this interruption to their way of life and he knew things would never be the same again, but he also knew it would take something very serious to make him change his views and join in their fight. That serious event was not long in coming.

Chapter Seventeen

At first the attacks on the drainage works had been sporadic and ill planned but gradually as the retaining banks grew and the marshes began to drain and dry out, the opposition hardened. Fen men from Deeping, Crowland and Cubbit combined their intelligence and their manpower to make concerted attacks on the diggings. Lovell's overseer asked for members of his workforce to man the banks overnight to keep the attackers at bay and protect the work. Skirmishes broke out regularly and injuries were sustained on both sides. Fighting sank into brawling with clubs and shovels used as weapons. The drainage workers and the fen men grew ever more angry at each other and bad blood split the villages. A few of the Deeping men were apprehended and finished up in front of the local magistrates and in gaol. In Cubbit, Bert Ward and his bully boys beat up men they suspected of being involved in the opposition.

Jake woke one night to the sounds of fighting close by his hut. By the time he was fully awake and had stealthily crept out into the darkness to see what was happening, all had gone quite again. He stood in the shadow of his hut wall and listened intently to the sounds of the night. Across the fen came the cry of a duck, disturbed from its sleep. From the village he could just make out the sounds of a group of men walking quickly away from him. He was about to walk back into his hut and get back to sleep when he heard a faint groaning sound from the darkened road somewhere between his hut and Annie's.

Jake went back into his hut and grabbed a stout branch he had gathered for his fire. Armed with this makeshift club, he walked silently towards the Owen's hut stopping every few steps to listen and to check the road. Suddenly he heard the groans again, this time they were much nearer.

Following the faint sounds, Jake looked down the bank from the raised roadway and onto the fen below. In the moonlight he saw a shadowy bundle in the ditch; a bundle that moved slightly and groaned!

Jake left the road and walked down the bank to the figure lying in the ditch. By the time he reached the man, he recognised him as Tom Skinner, the slodger who had asked to borrow the punt. He knelt down beside the man and raised him up to a sitting position. It was obvious Tom was injured badly by his laboured breathing and constant heavy groans.

"Come on Tom. Try to get up and I'll get you to my hut and the light of the fire. Then I can see what I can do for you."

Tom tried to raise himself but collapsed into Jake's arms. The young man lifted the injured man onto his shoulder and staggered up the bank to the road.

"Who's that? What's going on?" Annie's voice penetrated the night. She had been disturbed by the fighting and had looked out of her hut to see the shadowy figure of her neighbour and his companion.

"Its me, Jake. Come and give me a hand Annie. Someone's been injured badly."

Annie went back into her hut and emerged a few minutes later holding a rushlight that she had ignited from the embers of her fire. She held the spluttering light above her head and approached the two men cautiously

Jake said. "Here, take his other arm and help me get him to my hut." Between them they dragged the injured man to Jake's home where they lay him on the bed.

"Who is it? What's happened?" Annie was shocked at the man's appearance. Blood covered his face and his nose and lips were split and bruised.

"It's Tom Skinner, the man who asked to use your punt. He's been beaten up."

Annie held the rush light closer to the injured man and looked to see the extent of his injuries.

"I'll clean him up." Jake said. "There's still some hot water on my fire. I'll need some cloth. Can you help?"

Annie hurried off into the night to fetch what she could to help the casualty.

Jake, who had ignited his own rush light, brought it close to the man's face to check his injuries. He wiped the blood from his mouth and raised Tom's head to give him a drink of water.

The injured man drank the water then spat out two broken teeth.

"Who did this?" Jake asked as he cleaned up the other wounds.

"Bert Ward and his cronies."

"I might have guessed as much. I suppose you are involved with the wrecking gangs at the drainage works?"

Tom nodded.

"And why were you out so late tonight? Have you been over to the river bank tonight?"

"No" Tom hesitated. "I was meeting some of the Deeping men. They are planning a big attack for tomorrow night. There'll be a full moon and we'll tear down all their work. Some of us will be making use of your punt to get behind the guards and surprise them."

Annie and her son came into the hut just as this last remark was made. She shook her head at the casualty and told him to keep quiet while she tended to his face. Toby stood by and watched his mother clean the wounds and bind up the man's head to stop the bleeding.

"They can't do this to people!" Toby turned to Jake.

"They can and they will. While the wreckers are breaking the law and throwing down the banks as soon as they are raised, this sort of attack will be on the increase."

Toby snorted. "Can't you do anything, Jake. You were a soldier. You know how to fight."

Jake ignored the boy's plea and turned to Tom Skinner, who was showing signs of recovering. "You'll have a swollen lip and two black eyes in the morning, Tom. You'll be bruised all over. I think you'd better stay here overnight and get home safely in tomorrows daylight."

Annie took her son and went home to her bed leaving Jake making up his fire and preparing a temporary bed of dried reeds for himself.

Next morning at first light, Tom hobbled out of Jake's hut and made for his own home. Jake watched him make his painful way into the village. Even though he had been beaten up, Tom Skinner made it clear he was still set on attacking the river banks that very night.

Chapter Eighteen.

The next day, Jake went fishing on the upper reaches of the Welland, keeping well away from the busy workmen who were cutting new drains and making new river banks. He had a good day catching eels and fish. By evening he was ready for home. He pulled the punt up onto the bank at his usual mooring place and secured it to a nearby willow with a rope. On his mind was the thought that the boat might well be used by the disgruntled fen men that same night. He wondered if he would find it there the next time he needed it to fish.

As Jake walked across the marshes towards Cubbit, he was passed by several workmen making their way to the drainage works. Obviously they were going to guard their banks for they were armed with clubs and knives. He wondered if they suspected the attack on their work planned for that night. He shrugged his shoulders and resolved not to get involved. Things were getting very serious when men like Tom Skinner were attacked on the high road and left in a ditch even though he was nowhere near the diggings at the time.

At the Owen's hut he unloaded his catch and spoke with Annie. "Thanks for your help last night. Tom was badly beaten up."

"How is he today?" She asked.

"He got up at first light and walked home. He was a bit worse for wear, stiff and bruised, but he will be alright. It's lucky I heard the attack on him or he could have been in that ditch all night."

"Does he know who attacked him?"

"Oh yes. It was Bert Ward, and his cronies. They think Tom has been attacking the new river banks after dark."

"They could well be right. He did mention another attack was due tonight, didn't he? I thought I heard him say that when I came into your hut last night."

"I believe so." Jake stopped himself from saying anything further as he noticed Toby was intently eves dropping on them. He changed the subject abruptly. "I've had a good day. There should be plenty of eels and fish for the kedger when he calls."

"I'm expecting him tomorrow afternoon. I'll settle with you later." Annie got on with her cooking and Jake made for home to eat and rest after a busy day.

Later that same evening, after the sun had gone down and the moon had risen over the fen, Annie walked up to Jake's hut. She tapped on the door and shouted his name.

Jake, who was resting in front of the glowing embers of his fire, got up and let her in. He was surprised at the visit so late in the day. "What's the matter, Annie? Your dad alright is he?"

"Dad's fine. He's asleep as usual. No, it's Toby. He's gone out and I don't know where he could be. I'd hope to find him here with you. Have you seen him?"

Jake shook his head. "No. Not seen nor heard him, not since I left your place earlier."

Annie frowned and shook her head.

"What's going through your mind Annie? You look very concerned."

"He's been talking a lot about the wreckers and the new river banks. He knows there is to be an attack on the diggings tonight; he heard Tom Skinner say so. I hope he's not taken it into his head to join the men and attack the drainage workings. He's only a child. He's no idea what he's getting into."

Jake frowned. Toby had certainly taken a great interest in the plans to attack the river workings. "Would you like me to walk over the fen and see if I can find him?"

"Would you? Oh that would put my mind at rest if you could find him."

Jake put on his coat and boots and walked back with Annie to her home. There he left her and headed out over the fen towards his boat. The night had closed in over the marshes and the full moon was riding high, reflected in the numerous silvery pools and on the wet mud. Jake knew his way blindfold across the fens. It was a dangerous area for strangers to tread but local men like Jake, knew every patch of quicksand and boggy ground. Several times as he progressed towards the river he stopped to listen for the sounds of anyone moving over the marsh but his only companions were the water birds and the nocturnal animals, like the foxes and otters that were hunting after dark. Occasionally he passed a reed bed and disturbed a sleeping water bird that screeched its warning call as it flew into the darkness, but there was no sign of humans anywhere.

When he got to his usual mooring, Jake was surprised to see his boat had already gone. He assumed Tom Skinner had already taken it and gone on the river, probably to pick up some of the Deeping men who were joining them that night to attack the drainage workings. Jake stood a few minutes deciding what to do next. Finally he decided to walk along the riverside towards the new banks to see for himself what was happening. Nowhere was there any sign of Toby or the other Cubbit men.

As he approached the area where the new banks had been raised, Jake could see fires had been lit and many men were standing around them talking in low voices. He kept to the shadows and crept up on the guards as close as he dared without being seen or heard.

In the darkness above the low mumbling of voices he distinctly recognised the laughter of the fen reeve. With no sign of Toby and no intention of getting involved in the night's affairs, Jake turned away and made for home. He called in at Annie's hut to check if Toby had returned home and to tell her there was no sign of him on the fen.

"He's still not home. I'll leather him when he gets in." Annie was obviously very worried and angry at her son.

"I've been all along the river bank and over as far as your boat but he's nowhere to be seen." Jake didn't mention that the boat was missing as he knew this would only cause her more worry. "He's used to the fen, Annie. He's been all over it with me. He'll be alright, I'm sure." Jakes reassurance belied his real feelings but he could see nothing to be gained by upsetting the girl further.

Once back home Jake made up his fire and sat in the glow of it, drinking small beer and considering the night's events. There was bound to be a major confrontation at the new workings. The local slodgers and their Deeping allies were hell bent on ruining the new river banks. If they could undo all the work that Lovell's men had completed, time would run out for draining the fens before the autumn floods covered the area with water once again. For both sides of the argument these next few weeks would be crucial to the success or failure of the enterprise. His only hope was that Toby had the sense to stay out of trouble and not get involved. He drifted off to sleep considering the possibilities.

Early on the morning after Toby's disappearance, Annie knocked on Jake's hut door. He answered the knock and let her in. It was hardly necessary to ask her if her son had come home safely that night for her tired and haggard expression told it all.

"No sign of him then?"

"No. I sat up all night waiting for him but he's not returned home. I don't know what to do Jake." She burst into tears.

He put his arm around her heaving shoulders and patted her back.

"I'll go around the village and the fen and look for him. He's sure to be somewhere safe. Don't fret, I'll find him"

The girl left Jake's hut and headed home with tears still running down her cheeks.

Jake walked into Cubbit village and made for Tom Skinners house where he found the man repairing his fishing nets in the yard.

"Jake?" Tom looked up from his work at the approaching footsteps.

"Morning, Tom. Did you borrow the boat last night?"

"Yes, but I think it was put back after the attack."

"Thanks. Did you happen to see young Toby Owen last night?"

"Yes. As a matter of fact he was waiting at the boat for us. He certainly knows how to paddle that punt, he does."

"Did he come with you to attack the diggers?"

"No. I insisted he took the boat back up the river while we crept up on the guards. All hell broke loose then. You should have been there... we routed them and we threw down the new workings. We..."

Jake held up his hand and interrupted Tom in full flow. "Toby's not come home yet. His mother's worried to death about him. Any ideas where he might be?"

Tom stood up and thumped his fist on the top of barrel where he had been sitting. "I told him to stay in the boat in the middle of the river until he got back to your mooring."

"Tell me exactly what happened last night." Jake insisted.

"We took them completely by surprise by attacking them on two sides. Most of the men crept up over the fen but several of us used the boat to draw them the wrong way. We yelled and made a noise so they thought we were coming from the river, then the main body of men attacked from the fen. We outnumbered them two to one. They ran like rabbits. We put them to flight even though they had a gun."

"A gun?" Jake queried.

"One shot was fired by somebody on their side; that was all. We overwhelmed them before they could regroup. We dug up the new banks and let the tide flow out of the river then we threw all their tools into the water. I'm sure by now the river water will have finished our work and undone all of theirs."

"What about Toby? Where was he when all this was going on?"

"The last I saw of him he was in your boat and paddling out to the middle of the river. I assume he took the boat back and moored it."

"The boat is nowhere to be seen. Neither is Toby."

Tom just shrugged his shoulders; he had no more answers.

With a clearer idea of what had happened the previous night, Jake set off across the fen towards the new workings and the site of the previous night's scuffles. He had to make a series of detours because the river water had flooded much more of the low lying fen but he finally made it to the area where the attack had taken place. There were two men already there before him, surveying the damage to the new banks and estimating the situation. Lovell's overseer was deep in conversation with Bert Ward. From the men's expressions it was obvious the slodgers' night's work had dealt a serious blow to Lovell's plans to drain the area.

Bert Ward turned as Jake approached them. "What do you want? Come to see the damage you did last night?"

"No, I wasn't here last night and I have witnesses to prove it."

Ward took a menacing step towards Jake and sneered. "Come to gloat then at your mate's handiwork?"

Jake stood his ground. "No. I've come to look for a local child whose gone missing. Have you seen young Toby Owen?"

Ward shook his head emphatically and backed off. "I've got more pressing things to do than look for lost kids."

Jake ignore the reeve and addressed the overseer. "Do you mind if I look around for him. My boat is missing and he may have taken it."

"There's a boat over there on the far bank. Is that yours?"

Jake looked over the river and was relieved to see it was indeed his boat. He nodded.

"Well, that was used last night to sneak up on us." Ward grunted.

"It wasn't me, I can assure you. The boat was safely moored towards Crowland when I left it. Anyone could have taken it. It's not the first time it's been removed, as you well know."

"Look where you like." The overseer snapped. "We have better things to do."

Jake walked along the river bank where the fight had taken place the previous night. All around were signs of the struggle. Braziers were topple over leaving the smouldering ashes in heaps on the mud bank, sticks and ropes were strewn all over the area, there was even a knife discarded in the mud. Jake walked some distance from the two men along the mud bank looking for any sign of Toby but he found nothing. Disappointed at his lack of success, he turned back towards his boat. At least he could return that to its usual mooring place while he was on that stretch of the river.

To get to his boat Jake realised he would have to cross the river. He knew he had two choices: to walk into Spalding to cross the stone bridge there and return on foot on the opposite bank, or to try to wade and swim across where he was. The thought of three miles into the town and the same distance back to the punt decided his course of action for him. He would try to cross the river as the tide was low and he had no time to waste in his search for Toby.

Jake stripped off and walked into the Welland, holding his clothes above his head to keep them dry. The water was cold but once over the initial shock, he progressed slowly across the river bed, feeling his way with his bare feet. This plan worked well until he came to a part of the river where the bottom consisted of soft mud. He felt his feet sink into the mud and knew he would probably go under the surface. Taking a deep breath he struggled on, his arms held high above him to keep his clothes out of the water, but his face went under the surface. Luckily he soon found a firmer footing and managed to make it to the other bank with his clothes still relatively dry.

In a few minutes he had dressed again, stopped shivering and went to his punt to check if the paddle was still there. That was when he got a terrible shock. In the bottom of the boat was a still, small, figure laying face down. From the colour of the coat, Jake immediately recognised Toby!

Jake hesitated then stepped down into the boat and turned the boy over. It was at once obvious from his appearance that Toby was dead! The body was limp, his face was pale and grey. Jake froze, the boy still laying in his arms. Even though he had seen death many times before when he was fighting in the army, this time it was personal, this time it was Toby, the boy he had grown to know and like.

Jake sat for some time nursing the limp body coming to terms with the terrible truth that he would have to break the news to the boy's mother. When he had gathered his wits, Jake gently lay the body on its back in the bottom of the boat. It was then he saw the gaping wound in Toby's chest. Blood had seeped onto the boy's shirt and coat from the wound. Jake took a second look at the injury and immediately recognised it was the result of a lead ball penetrating the boy's chest. Toby had been shot! Tears sprung to the battle hardened soldier's eyes. This was not just men rioting over mud banks, it was murder!

Jake slowly paddled the boat across the Welland and drove the prow into the mud bank near where the reeve and the overseer where standing, deep in conversation. He shouted angrily to attract their attention.

"You two, take at look at this. This is murder. Someone used a gun last night during those riots. Firing a firearm in the dark must be tantamount to murder."

The two men stopped instantly their conversation and walked to the boat.

"It's Toby, the boy I was searching for. He's just a young lad and now he's dead. Who would use a gun in the dark when men are fighting. It was a terrible thing to do."

The two men stood shocked into silence. The overseer shook his head in disbelief. He turned to Bert Ward and asked. "Did any of your men have a gun?"

Bert was emphatic. "No. What labourer can afford a gun." He hesitated then pointedly said to Jake. "You are the only local man I know of who has a gun. Were you here last night?"

Jake was shocked at the insinuation. "You know full well I reported my gun as stolen some time ago."

"Ah! So you say." Bert shook his head.

Jake was incensed. "With my army training, I'd have more sense than to fire a gun in the dark and into a crowd of people."

Ward shook his head slowly and stood tightlipped and silent, but his whole manner was accusing. When he did speak he said, "I don't recall you telling me anything about your gun being stolen."

Jake was shocked. That was a blatant lie. He stood up in the boat and shook his fist at the reeve. "You have a convenient memory. It's a good job I reported the theft at the time to the Spalding magistrates and the tradesmen in the town, isn't it."

Ward just looked at his feet and remained silent.

The overseer could see things were getting heated so he took charge of the situation. He placed himself between the two men.

"We'll have to report this to the magistrates in Spalding. There'll be an enquiry of course. You'd better leave the boy where he is until the magistrate has seen him. Then we'll get the body back to Cubbit'. I'll ride into town right now to report the death."

Jake nodded agreement and sat back in his boat next to Toby's. He was in shock and unable to think straight. But he realised it would fall to him to break the terrible news to Annie and her father. That was a sad task he did not want but he couldn't avoid it. He looked down at the dead boy's face and tears welled up in his eyes. Annie would be devastated.

Chapter Nineteen

As Jake walked the fen from the drainage works to Cubbit, his mind was in turmoil. How could he tell Annie that her son was dead, shot in the chest at the previous night's riot? He rehearsed how he would break the tragic news as he trudged across the marsh but arrived at the village far too soon and without a clue how he could break such news gently.

Annie was standing at her front door, arms folded and stony faced as she watched Jake walk along the main road towards her. He was alone, that much was clear, so he had not found Toby and he walked as if he had the black dog on his back. She ran to greet him and ask the news.

"Any sign of him, Jake?"

Jake didn't answer but took her by her arm and led her back to her shack.

"Jake? What's the matter?"

Once inside her home, Jake held her tightly in his arms and broke the news to her. "Toby is dead. I found his body in the boat on the river."

Annie burst into tears and screamed. She beat Jake's chest with her fists and violently shook her head, denying what he had told her.

For several minutes, Jake stood stoically under her onslaught, waiting for her to calm down. After a few minutes she collapsed in his arms and asked, between sobs. "How?...How Jake? Did he drown?"

"No..."Jake hesitated. There was no easy way to break the awful news..."He was shot during last night's attack on the river banks."

"Shot!" Annie screamed the word and pushed Jake away.

Charlie Owen, who had been asleep on his bed, woke up with a start. "Is Toby home?" He asked.

"No dad. He's dead. He'll never come home again." She rushed over, encircled the old man in her arms and they cried together.

Jake stood just inside the doorway, tears running down his face. He had rehearsed this moment many times as he walked from the river but the reality was far worse than he'd ever imagined. A mother's loss of her only son was more than he could bear to witness. He stepped outside and stood with his back against the shack wall, clenching and unclenching his fists, the tears still coursing down his cheeks.

After some time, Annie peered out of the doorway and asked him to come back into the house to explain in full what he had found.

"Tell me everything, Jake. Every detail. I want to know all there is to know."

Jake sat beside her and held her hand. "I found him in the bottom of my boat. He was cold and had obviously been killed the night before. I'm told someone had a firearm and fired it indiscriminately into the crowd of men while they were fighting last night. I understand there was only one shot fired and it was dark, so the person who used the gun would have no idea who he had hit."

Annie sobbed quietly as she listened.

Jake continued. "Toby was in my boat on the river when the shot was fired. The lad was in the wrong place at the wrong time. No one knew he had been shot until I found him this morning."

"If only he'd not gone out." Annie sobbed. "I should have stopped him."

"How could you? He didn't ask your permission, did he?"

"No. He just went his own way."

"It's an awful tragedy, Annie but you cannot be blamed for it. It was an accident."

"An accident? More like murder! You said yourself, who would shoot a gun into a crowd in the middle of the night?"

"I don't know. But there will be an enquiry. Lovell's overseer has ridden into Spalding to inform the magistrate and the constable will come over to investigate."

"Where is Toby now?"

"I had to leave him in the boat at the scene of his death until the magistrate has seen him."

Once more Annie burst into tears and clung to Jake.

Charlie Owen, brought to his senses by the terrible news, made a supreme effort and sat up on his bed. "They must find out who did this. Someone must pay for my boy's young life."

Jake sat staring at the reed strewn floor, unable to suggest anything that would ease their pain. Toby was gone. The light had gone out of their lives.

Later that day Lovell's overseer called on Annie to tell her the investigation at the river was completed and she could retrieve Toby's body.

"There will be an investigation held at the church. The magistrate will let you know about that. Can I say how sorry we are that your son has been killed."

Annie took the news in silence. Apologies and investigations would not bring Toby back to life. She told Jake the body could be collected.

Jake, with the help of Tom Skinner and a few of his mates, carried Toby home across the fen. When they arrived at the Owen's cottage the kedger was there. Jake rushed to help Annie deal with the man, fearing she couldn't cope, but he need not have bothered for she seemed fully capable of selling him the catch.

"Are you alright?" Jake enquired, surprised at her composure.

"I'm fine." Annie shook her head at him. "Don't fuss me. There's nothing can be done about Toby now. We will have to get on with our lives without him."

Jake backed away and let her deal with the kedger while Tom and the other men carried Toby's body into the hut. He realised she must still be in shock from the ordeal but he knew he must let her deal with her loss in her own way. All he could do was stand by to support her if she needed it. He was suspicious she was in denial about her son's death but when he went back into the hut he found her standing beside the body, dry eyed and smiling.

"He was a lovely lad, wasn't he Jake."

Jake just nodded, unable to find any words of comfort to give her.

Annie folded her dead son's arms across his chest and placed a sheet over him, then she sat on the floor and worked on one of her willow eel traps as if nothing had happened.

Charlie Owen took Toby's death to heart. He sat on his bed and cried incessantly. "Why…why…why my son?"

Jake went over to comfort the old man. "Your grandson was …" He got no further.

"Toby was not my grandson he was my son. Don't you understand? I have lost my only son."

Jake didn't understand and didn't know what to say.

Annie put down her work and put her arm around her father. "Yes dad, he was our son, but he's gone now."

Jake stood by her while she lulled the old man back to sleep. Finally, when she had succeeded in getting him to relax and close his eyes she moved closer to her neighbour.

"He's taken it bad, Annie. He's delirious thinking he's Toby's father."

Annie shook her head and whispered. "Come outside, Jake, I've something to tell you."

Out in the fresh air the couple stood against the hut wall. Jake looked at her questioningly. Whatever she was going to tell him, seemed very important by her serious manner and the way she had spoken of it.

Annie drew in a long breath and reached out for Jake's hands. "My father was the man who raped me when I was just a girl."

Jake frowned, and made to speak but she placed a finger on his lips to silence him.

"I've known all along. He called out my mother's name that night. She had died a short time before and he was drunk. I recognised his voice in my ear. People tell me I looked like my mother and he thought I was her."

Jake turned over this confession in his mind, finally he said. "So that's how you knew the crippled lad hadn't raped you."

She nodded.

"Why did you stay with him?"

"Where else had I to go? I had a baby who needed a loving home. He seemed to be unaware of what had happened at the time. But he must have realised soon afterwards because he treated Toby like his own son, in all but name."

"How could you forgive him, raping you when you were just a child?"

Annie smiled. "He was and still is my father, my only living relative. He was drunk and mistaken. That's all there is to it."

"And it was never mentioned during all these years?"

"No. If I had raised the question our lives would have never been the same. I suppose we lived a lie but that way was better for all of us."

She looked questioningly up at Jake. "This doesn't effect the way you and I get on, does it? Do you think any the less of me for living a lie all these years?"

Jake looked down at her pleading face and pulled her towards him, holding her head against his chest, he buried his fingers in her long brown hair. "No. I think you have been very sensible. I can see now that nothing would have been gained by bringing this into the open. Certainly, Toby's life would have been blighted and your family life would have been shattered."

Annie led Jake back into the hut where her father was still asleep, snoring loudly on his bed. "I will have to arrange a funeral for Toby. Tomorrow I'll go and see the curate and talk to him about it."

Jake was surprised how well she seemed to be coping with the boy's death. Annie was a small girl but she was far from the delicate person he'd imagined her to be. There was a steely strength in her that belied her usual manner and appearance.

"I'd like to lay him to rest next to my mother in the churchyard. If I can afford the cost of it."

Jake saw at last a way he could help. "Keep my share of the kedger's money, Annie. You need it more than me."

Annie burst into tears. That simple act of kindness proved too much for her to bear. The floodgates opened and she sobbed her heart out; all her pent up feelings came out in a rush. Jake could only hold her close to him waiting for the sobbing to subside.

Chapter Twenty.

Toby's funeral was held in the morning at the village church, three days after his death. Annie and Jake were the main mourners as Charlie Owen was too ill to leave his bed, but most of the village turned out to pay their respects. The local men who had been at the riverbank that fateful night, as well as Bert Ward and the drainage workers attended the service. The curate, Martin Somerscal, preached a sermon condemning the way the wreckers were holding up the fen drainage, but everyone had expected that as it was well known he sided with the Spalding gentry who stood to gain from the reclaimed marshland.

Annie bore the service stoically. She shed no more tears for her son, but she did lean heavily on Jake's arm as they lowered his body into the ground and covered it with soil. Jake couldn't hold back a few tears, as much for her as for the boy.

Molly Kettle stopped them as they left the churchyard. "I'm so sorry, Annie. I've known your lad from being a baby. He was a credit to you. It was tragic the way he was brought into this world and tragic the way he left it."

Annie and Jake walked to her home where she made a meal and comforted her father. The three of them ate in silence, each one lost in their own thoughts and memories of Toby. Jake was surprised how well Annie seemed to be taking the death of her son. She had hidden strengths that he would not have expected in one so young and fragile looking. The most tears were shed by Charlie Owen, who lay on his sickbed and sobbed.

A week after the funeral the coroner in Spalding held an enquiry into the death. The coroner called a jury of twenty three local men of good standing to ascertain if a trial should be held by the Justice of the Peace. There were not many of the Cubbit villagers present; only the few who had been summoned to give evidence.

Annie and Jake were among this small group, as was Bert Ward and Lovell's overseer. Non of the wreckers were present. They had remained anonymous for their own safety, as they were regarded as criminals in the eyes of the law. When the coroner arrived he was accompanied by Thomas Lovell who seemed to be very friendly with the official.

After the constable had described how he found the body, Annie was called to speak as the first witness.

"You are Annie Owen, the dead boy's mother?"

"Yes Sir." She stood upright and dry eyed, her voice loud and firm.

Jake watched her with growing admiration; she was coping well with this awful situation. He could not put himself in her shoes and understand how she felt but he knew he would not be so composed.

"Do you know why your son left home that night?"

"No Sir."

"Do you think he knew about the proposed attack on the drainage site?"

"I don't know, Sir." Annie lied. "We live quiet and busy lives, earning our living. I don't know what he had heard in the village or from his friends."

Thomas Lovell, who was sitting close by the coroner's magistrates table leaned over and whispered something to him.

"Can you think of any other reason why Toby Owen would be at the river bank that night?"

"No Sir. He did visit the area when he went fishing but that was usually with my neighbour, Jake Fowler. I would never have allowed him to go out alone at night to fish, if he'd told me what he intended to do."

"Thank you Miss Owen. I can see you loved your son. We can only say how sorry we are this awful thing has happened to him."

Annie lowered her eyes and looked down at her feet.

The coroner continued. "Please stand down for the moment but stay in the court in case he have other questions to ask you." Then he thanked her once again for giving her evidence so clearly in such regrettable circumstances

Next the coroner called Jake Fowler to stand before him and give his version of events. After identifying himself and swearing to be truthful, Jake was questioned.

"Jake Fowler, tell us how you became involved in this death."

"I was asked to look for the lad by his mother. We are neighbours, Sir. She was getting very worried about him being out so late and out on his own. She came to my home and asked me to help find him."

"Why did you go particularly to search at the drainage site? Where you expecting to find him there?"

"I actually looked all over the fen where I knew Toby usually went. I went to the drainage site only as part of my searches, Sir."

"I understand you found the body in your boat."

"Yes Sir."

"Why would the boy be in your boat?"

"The boat actually belongs to Toby's family. Charlie Owen, Toby's grandfather, lets me use it to fish. I have often taken Toby with me on fishing expeditions so he was familiar with the boat, the river and the mooring place, Sir."

The coroner nodded he understood and held a whispered conversation with his clerk and then with Thomas Lovell. Turning back to Jake he continued with a very direct question.

"Were you involved in the throwing down of the drainage banks that night?"

There was an audible gasp from a one of the watching villagers. It was obvious this enquiry was being used to persecute the wreckers and not just to ascertain the method of Toby's death..

"No, Sir." Jake drew himself upright and stared straight ahead as he had on parade in his army days. "I have witnesses to prove that, Sir."

The coroner looked down at his notes. "Tell me how you found the body?"

"I was talking to the reeve and his overseer when I saw my boat marooned on the other side of the river, lodged on the bank."

"Were you looking for this boat at the time?"

"Yes Sir. When I searched for Toby and I found the boat had been taken I knew there was a chance he had taken it to fish. I was searching for both the boy and the boat."

"Why would he have taken it? Did he often fish at night on his own?"

"I don't know why he took it .He didn't usually fish on his own, Sir."

"What did you think when you found the boat near the place the riots took place?"

"When I saw the boat I assumed it had broken free from its mooring and floated downstream. I waded across to get it then found Toby's body laying inside it. His body was hidden out of sight until I got right up to the boat."

The coroner stroked his chin and considered his next question carefully. "I understand the boy was shot with a firearm. Witnesses have said they heard the sound of a gunshot during the riots that night. In your daily visits to the marshes you must see what goes on there. Do you know of anyone possessing a firearm?"

"No, Sir. Most of the slodgers net and trap. Firearms are expensive and out of the reach of ordinary working men."

"But you posses a firearm, I am told." He glanced over at the jury to make sure they were paying attention.

Jake looked across at Bert Ward who was studiously looking at his feet, avoiding any eye contact. "I no longer have the matchlock gun I bought with me from the army. It was stolen some time ago. I did report it to the fen reeve at the time, Sir."

Again the coroner consulted his notes. "It seems the reeve cannot confirm that."

"Then you must consult your magistrates in Spalding, Sir, because I reported it there the same day that I told the reeve. I also reported it to the smith and to Johnny Acres in case they came across it." Jake turned to look pointedly at Bert Ward. "The reeve seems to have a very poor memory."

The coroner consulted his clerk once again then dismissed Jake with a wave of his hand. "That's all for now. Stay here in case we have further need to question you."

Bert Ward was the next to be called. "You are the fen reeve for the village of Cubbit?"

"Yes Sir."

"Tell us about the night when the boy was killed."

"I was on duty guarding the new riverbanks, Sir. We were expecting trouble and we got it. We were set upon by a gang of wreckers. Men from Cubbit and from Deeping attacked us."

"Did you recognise any of the men?"

"No Sir. They had plastered their faces with mud to disguise themselves."

"Then how can you say they were Cubbit and Deeping men?"

Bert looked embarrassed and stared down at his feet.

The constable continued. "You say there was just one single gun shot."

"Yes, Sir."

"Did you hear the gunshot?"

"Yes Sir. It came from the direction of Crowland, from upriver, Sir. I'm sure one of our attackers fired it at us."

"Do you know of anyone in this area that owns a firearm?

"Only Jake Fowler, Sir."

Lovell's overseer was the next witness called. He confirmed most of what the reeve had said except he wasn't sure which direction the gunshot came from.

"I was too busy defending myself to notice where the sound came from, Sir. There were men all over the place fighting and shouting, and it was dark."

The coroner stopped the inquest for lunch but told the witnesses they must come back that afternoon in case he wanted to speak to them again to answer any queries. With a sigh of relief Annie walked out of the hall and waited for Jake.

Jake was in no hurry to leave the proceedings he wanted to speak to Bert Ward to remind him of the occasion he had reported the theft of his gun. Ward tried to avoid the younger man but Jake cornered him by the main doorway.

"How come you have conveniently forgotten my reporting the theft of that matchlock gun?"

The reeve tried to turn away from his questioner. Jake stood his ground and said

"I think you're up to something. I think you are trying to put suspicion onto me to save someone else's skin."

Ward shook his head emphatically.

Jake stared him straight in the eye and exclaimed. "I'll be watching you! You're definitely up to something fishy."

The confrontation over, Jake joined Annie and they walked together into the town centre where they bought refreshments at a local inn. As they sat together. Jake raised the question of the gun once again. "I really do not have a gun, Annie. I have no idea who stole it or even if it was my gun that killed Toby."

Annie took hold of his hand and squeezed it. "I know. You told me at the time it had been taken. Anyway you were nowhere near the riverbank the night Toby was killed; we both know that. Don't blame yourself for any of it. It was no fault of yours."

After the lunch break, the enquiry was reconvened. The coroner's clerk stood up before the court and read through the evidence they had gathered. The jury were then sent into an adjacent room to ponder on their verdict. It did not take them long to come to their decision.

The coroner announced the findings. "The only conclusion we can come to is that Toby Owen's death was accidental, caused by a gunshot wound of unknown origin. It seems it is impossible to ascertain who fired that shot. In these circumstances there is no case to be sent to the Justice's court."

There was a murmur of disappointment from the listeners but most of them had expected such a verdict. The jury were drawn from well to do people in the area, farmers and gentry. These were the very people who would gain most from the drainage of the fen and would not want anything to delay the work of draining it. It appeared that Thomas Lovell had got his way.

Before the court adjourned, the coroner took the opportunity to condemn the attacks on the drainage works. He made it clear that anyone breaking the law by attacking Lovell's drainage workings must expect to be resisted, and they would be prosecuted if they were found to be at fault. In conclusion he said, "King James himself has authorised this drainage scheme. It is imperative it goes ahead with all haste before the winter floods set in."

Then Thomas Lovell stood up and addressed the court. "If we can complete the drainage works before the winter, the land will recover and be dry enough to plough by next summer. We could do with more helpers to build the sluice gates and the drainage engines. Any volunteers would be most welcome."

The enquiry over, the people drifted out of the courtroom and stood in small groups discussing the findings. Annie and Jake walked back to Cubbit to tell her father what had been said. He took the news badly.

"Someone kills my boy and no one is to blame!" He started to cry again, turning his face to the wall and sobbing uncontrollably. Even Annie could not console him.

Jake stood by in silence and watched the family try to cope with their son's death. It seemed to him that Charlie had given up wanting to live. It did not bode well for the old man's fight against the ague.

Chapter Twenty One

The drainage works on Deeping fen went on at an increasing pace as the autumn approached. Lovell brought in hundreds more men to dig the new dykes, to build wooden sluice gates to control the flow of the water off the land, and to erect the wind pumps that lifted the water from the fen into the river. He had worked on the continent and had experience of such matters. He employed Dutch workmen to build the small wind driven pumps at strategic junctions of the drains and the river, to lift the water off the low lying land.

Small groups of local men opposed to the drainage kept trying to throw down the workings but they were fighting a losing battle. Eventually a secret meeting was called of all those opposed to the work. Disgruntled men from Cubbit, Deeping and all the surrounding villages combined to plan a last ditch attempt to ruin the plans before it was too late. Winter was approaching; the time of year the fens flooded from the tidal flow of water from the sea and from the rain water draining down from inland. This was the best time to undo all of Lovell's work, and it was the best time to prevent him carrying on with it.

Jake heard about the meeting from Tom Skinner and decided to go along to hear what was being proposed. He was still reluctant to give his whole hearted support to the wreckers but Toby's death had raised doubts in his mind about the people protecting the workings. He felt he owed it to Toby to find out who had used a gun and to settle the score with him. The major attack being planned could provide him with the cover he needed to find out who was behind the killing.

The night the wreckers chose was the night of a full moon and a high tide. Fortunately there was a heavy cloud cover that night so their movements were well hidden. They knew they had a difficult job on their hands because the security at the main sites on the river was much tighter than it had ever been before.

Lovell paid good money to have his works protected as the end of the scheme approached. He had much to gain from the completion of the scheme but everything to lose if it failed at that late hour as he had sunk all of his personal fortune into the scheme.

The disgruntled slodgers split into several groups. Some went to tear down the new wooden sluice gates. Others went to destroy the wind pumps, but the main body of men went to attack the new river banks, to destroy them and allow the river water to flow back onto the fens. They knew that once the banks were breached the water would do the rest of their work by gushing through and taking the new banks with it.

Jake kept his own counsel and made his way alone to his boat, which was moored upriver from the main attack. He sat in the punt waiting and listening to the sounds of the night, the water lapping against the boat side and the occasional cry of water birds disturbed in their sleep. Eventually he heard the unmistakable cries and shouts of men fighting, signalling the attacks had started. It was time for him to paddle downstream towards the noise. Silently, he paddled his boat past groups of wreckers pulling the new sluice gates down and attacking the wind pumps. One wooden pump house was already on fire, lighting the area around it with the dancing flames and throwing an arc of light across the river. As he passed the area, Jake paddled his punt near the far bank to avoid being seen. He remained on that far side of the river until he had gone by the main body of men fighting then he ran the boat into the bank and approached the fighting from the rear and on foot, taking care to remain undetected.

Jake was experienced in hand to hand fighting. He smeared his face with mud to camouflage himself and took his knife and a cudgel in his hands. The main fighting was going on ahead of him as he was approaching Lovell's men from behind. He hoped no one would expect him to be there.

In the light of a single brazier, Jake saw the burley figure of Bert Ward, standing back from the action but exhorting his men to fight off the intruders. Jake crept up to the brazier, keeping a low profile by keeping near the water's edge; he stayed down the river bank and below eye level. When he was level with the brazier he crawled up the bank and peered over the edge to see what was going on. Luckily Lovell's men were occupied with the intruders and no one was looking in Jake's direction.

In the light of the fire Jake noticed something that made his heart race. Laying on the ground lightly covered by a piece of sacking, was a gun! It was a gun that looked very much like the one he had lost. Suddenly the fighting moved in his direction. Ward and his men were beaten back to the brazier and the struggle came very close to where Jake was hiding. He ducked his head down and waited for the fighting to move away again. Curses and cries rent the air as men fought furiously with clubs and shovels. Slowly Ward's men got the upper hand and the wreckers were beaten back.

As soon as the action moved away again, Jake peered above the riverbank to check if the firearm was still there; finding it was, he crawled up the bank and crept towards the sacking and the gun. Taking the matchlock in his hands he felt the along stock, searching with his fingers for the initials he had carved into the wood. Sure enough, the imprint was still there! The carved letters JF could be felt and seen when he held the stock up to the light of the fire.

It was his stolen gun and from the weight of it in his hands, he knew it had been left loaded and ready for use. He checked the pan and saw it had black powder in it. It was definitely ready to fire. Someone had left the gun primed and loaded with black powder and shot!

Jake considered the situation. He was certain there wasn't another matchlock in the Cubbit fen. His was the only one. Now he felt certain that this gun had been used to kill Toby. Reluctantly he decided to leave the gun where it was; to take it back into his possession and be seen with it, could lead people to believe he had used it on the night Toby Owen was shot. As he couldn't bring himself to reclaim the weapon and use it to shoot wildfowl on the fens, he decided to make it unusable. He took a handful of heavy grey clay from the damp river bank, quickly worked it into balls in his fingers and pushed them down the gun barrel, using the ram rod to make sure they were driven well home, then he replaced the gun where he had found it. The spiking of the gun completed, Jake crept back to his hiding place down the riverbank and waited to see who would return to pick the weapon up.

The fighting continued for a long time. Jake could hear the sounds of men shouting in the distance. Gradually they seemed to be coming nearer to him. He waited patiently to see who would own the gun for he knew the person who had it would not leave it to be found by anyone else. Eventually his patience was rewarded. A large figure loomed out of the darkness and approached the glowing brazier. The man threw a few more sticks onto the fire, which by then was only glowing embers. After a few minutes the kindling caught fire and leapt into life. Flames lit up the darkness and the figure silhouetted again the light. Jake watched as the man took a glowing stick from the fire, picked up the matchlock gun and applied the flame to the end of slow fuse.

With the gun primed for action the man's turned towards Jake. At last his face was illuminated by the fire. It was Bert Ward! The reeve seemed to be waiting to use the gun if the fighting came even nearer. Jake stood up and challenged him.

"Ward! I see you have my stolen gun. Did you murder Toby Owen with it?"

Bert Ward swiftly turned around, startled by the shout. He immediately recognised the figure challenging him and exclaimed. "Oh it's you! I might have known you'd be involved in tonight's wrecking It's time you got what you deserve." He lifted the gun to his shoulder and took aim at Jake.

Jake's head swam with memories of the shot he'd taken in his shoulder in Ireland but he stood his ground even though all his worst nightmares had suddenly become reality. Instinct and training cried out for him to drop down the riverbank and out of sight but he stood firm and defiant, barely twelve feet away from barrel of the gun.

Bert Ward quickly sighted along the gun barrel and pulled the trigger.

Jake heard the click as the trigger was pulled and saw the glowing end of the fuse arc towards the pan. There was a small flash as the charge ignited. Instinctively he turned his head away from the blast and raised his arms to shield his face. There was a slight sound as the fuse ignited the black powder in the pan, immediately followed by a loud explosion as the main charge of black powder ignited inside the gun.

With a blinding flash of light, the barrel of the matchlock blew into a dozen pieces and exploded in Bert Ward's hands. A few tiny fragments of hot steel and gunpowder reached Jake and burned holes in his coat sleeves. The embers glowed on his clothes and the smell of scorching filled his nostrils but the lead ball didn't hit him.

The clay he had rammed into the gun barrel had blocked it completely and contained the explosion. The gun blew up in his assailant's face.

When Jake uncovered his eyes he saw Bert Ward laying on the ground, kicking and screaming, covering his face with his hands. Blood poured from between the injured man's fingers and down his wrists, his hair and coat were glowing and smoking where they had caught fire and burned.

Jake brushed the embers from his coat, walked to the brazier and stood over the reeve. He watched as the man stopped writhing on the ground and fell silent. In the light from the blazing brazier, he saw a sliver of steel from the gun barrel had pierced one of Ward's eyes and had entered his head, piercing his brain like a sharp stiletto. In a matter of minutes Bert Ward was dead.

Jake left the body and the scene of the riots the way he had come. He pushed his punt into the river and climbed into it. In the bottom of the boat was a spare eel trap, which he had intended to place in the river. He set the willow trap in the Welland, opposite the brazier and the body of the reeve, knowing that would give him a good excuse to visit the site the next day.

As Jake paddle upstream to his usual mooring place, he felt a grim satisfaction at avenging Toby's death. He kept his boat on the far side of the Welland, in the darkness and well away from the riots, which were still going on, as he didn't wish to be seen in the area. Judging by the debris strewn everywhere, the slodgers had had a successful night. He paddled his boat by the burning remains of the wooden wind pumps, which were only recently erected to pump the water from the new drains and into the river. Jake saw that every one of the new wooden sluice gates had been removed. Those that weren't set alight were floating down the river on the outgoing tide.

The Deeping men and their accomplices had done a thorough job of ruining the drainage works. Thomas Lovell's work was mostly undone.

Next morning Jake rose at his usual time and had breakfast. He trudged across the fen, making several detours to avoid the newly flooded areas where the river waters had reclaimed the marsh. Already there were signs of Lovell's men on the river banks, assessing the damage wrought by the slodgers the night before. Jake took his time paddling the boat down river to where he had set the single eel trap. When he arrived at the place, he could see several men standing near the burned our brazier, pointing along the riverbank and talking in low voices. One of them, a Cubbit man he had often seen with Bert Ward at the beer house, noticed him retrieving his eel trap and shouted over to him.

Jake checked the trap and finding it empty, replaced it in the river, then he paddle his boat over to the far bank where the man was standing waiting for him.

"What's a matter?" Jake asked

"You're local. Were you involved in the riots last night?"

Jake shook his head. He looked up at the group around the brazier and saw that the overseer and Thomas Lovell himself were among the men. He ran the boat prow hard into the bank and climbed out to join them.

"It's a bad business. The reeve's dead and our work is all undone." The Cubbit man told him.

Jake walked over to the men who were standing around the Ward's body. They parted as he approached.

"Oh dear!" Jake shook his head. "Did he get attacked last night?"

"He appears to have been shot in the face." The overseer said.

Jake bent down and picked up the remains of his stolen gun from beside the body. He turned the stock over in his hands to reveal the initials carved on it then he held the firearm up for all to see the split barrel.

"I have some experience of war. This gun has exploded. Looking at that man's face he must have been firing it at the time."

Lovell nodded agreement. He had seen action in battle as a young man and had already recognised the cause of the accident. "He probably overdid the black powder charge."

Jake didn't answer but held the gun stock up for all to see. "This was my matchlock gun; the one that was stolen. You may remember the magistrate made great play on it at the recent enquiry. Those are my initials carved on the but – JF, standing for Jake Fowler- I carved them there myself. I believe you have found the gun that murdered Toby Owen, and you have found the man who did it." He looked down at Bert Ward's inert body.

The group fell silent, digesting this new turn of events.

Jake took the initiative and broke into their thoughts. "It strikes me he was using that gun again last night during the riots. It's a miracle someone else wasn't killed." He threw the useless remains of the broken gun onto the ground beside the body. "In my opinion, he deserves what he got."

Jake left the men to report the death and the circumstances to the authorities in Spalding while he paddled his boat back upstream to his moorings. He had grown tired of seeing death while he was fighting with Robert Devereux's men but this death had been personal and he had few regrets. When Jake had moored the boat, he walked back to Cubbit and called on Annie to tell her the news.

"We now know almost for certain who shot your son, Annie." He held her hands tightly in his as he spoke to her.

She disengaged her fingers and stepped away from him. "Who?"

"Bert Ward has been found dead with my stolen gun. It seems he used it once too often last night during the riots and it blew up in his face."

The girl didn't answer, but Jake noticed a single tear running down her cheek. She turned away from him to hide her distress at this reminder of her loss, lowered her head and carried on sorting willow wands into bundles. Jake stood motionless in the doorway and watched her for several minutes, finally he turned and made his way to Molly Kettle's house where he ordered a tankard of beer and sat alone in her front room, drinking and considering the night's events.

Molly joined him in her parlour. "You alright, Jake? I don't remember seeing you drinking in here during the daytime. You look very thoughtful."

Jake nodded and smiled briefly at her. "I've just come from the river. There was a death during the riots last night."

"Oh! No one local, I hope?"

"Bert Ward. He seems to have killed himself using my stolen gun."

"Good God!" Molly sat down heavily beside him. "How come he was using a gun?"

"You know I had a gun I brought back from the Irish wars; they made great play on it at the enquiry into Toby's death. It was stolen soon after I moved into the village. It seems the reeve had it and it proved to be the death of him. It blew up in his face when he tried to fire it last night."

Molly looked shocked then very thoughtful. She looked Jake straight in the eye and raised her eyebrows in question.

Jake nodded. He knew what she was thinking. Old Molly was nobody's fool. "Yes. I came to the same conclusion. There are no other guns in this area.. The locals can't afford such luxuries. It's almost certain that gun killed Toby Owen."

Molly crossed herself. "God sometimes moves in mysterious ways."

Jake drained his mug and got up to leave.

"Have you told Annie?"

"Yes."

"It will not bring Toby back to her but there may be some consolation in knowing justice has now been done."

Jake walked home and lay on his bed contemplating the events of the last twenty four hours. He relived the moment Ward had pointed the gun at him and pulled the trigger. The risk he had taken and the horror of the situation crowded in on him. He burst into sobs, his body shaking with the strength of his feelings. It was a heavy price to pay but he had faced his demons and he had avenged Toby Owen.

Chapter Twenty Two

The news of Bert Ward's death soon spread through the village like a summer fire on the dry fen reed beds. The locals could be seen discussing it in groups of twos and threes at their front doors and in the churchyard. It was the talk of the alehouse. Tom Skinner sought out Jake when he heard that he had seen the body. He tapped on Jake's door.

"Come in" Jake called out, not bothering to get up from his bed.

Tom stepped into the hut and sat down beside the young man. "Is it true Bert Ward shot himself last night?"

"More or less."

Tom shook his head in disbelief. "He actually shot himself?" he queried.

"Not exactly. Ward was firing a matchlock gun when it blew up in his face. He was probably trying to shoot one of the rioters at the time"

Tom shook his head again, unable to comprehend what had happened.

"Ward had my stolen gun. The remains of it were still there beside his body."

"Oh! You saw his body? It must be true then."

"I happened to be in that area of the river this morning. Lovell and his men had found his body beside a brazier where he would have been protecting the new riverbanks last night."

"I know you weren't involved in last night's riots. We had a successful night. Most of the new banks are now broken down, the wind machines are burned and the new sluice gates have gone on the tide. That should stop Lovell and his mad schemes."

Jake smiled. "That's good. I did see the area the water has reclaimed when I went fishing this morning, but don't be surprised if they replace the banks and sluices before the winter sets in."

Tom grimaced. "I would expect them to, but we haven't finished yet. The Deeping slodgers are set on finishing the job and making sure the whole fens flood this winter as they always have. We haven't finished the job yet but we will."

Jake patted Tom on his shoulder. "You're doing a good job. I only hope you succeed."

Tom left and walked back towards the village, intent on sharing the details of the reeve's death with his friends and neighbours.

Jake sat on his bed and mused over the recent events. His gun had caused so much trouble and heartache in the village. If he hadn't brought it with him Toby would still be alive; if he hadn't taken it to the smith in Spalding and had it repaired it could not have been used in anger; if he had hidden it better it could not have been stolen. Jake was not normally a man given to worrying about things he could not alter but he felt responsible to Annie for her son's fate and was blaming himself. He lay back on his bed and stared at the rush ceiling. Maybe it would be wiser to leave the area and start afresh somewhere where he was not known, irrespective of the outcome of the fen drainage scheme. He felt Cubbit was no longer the place for him. He was contemplating how and where he should move when he heard hurried footsteps outside his door and a loud tapping to attract his attention.

"Come in" Expecting more questions from curious locals, he didn't bother to get up from his bed.

Annie rushed into the hut, breathless and flustered. "Dad's taken a turn for the worse." She blurted out her bad news.

Jake jumped up and put his arm around her narrow shoulders.

He patted her on her back and reassured her. "I'll come and keep you company. We'll see how he fares." They hurried back to the Owen's shack to check on Charlie.

Jake leaned over the old man, who was breathing noisily, making a rattling noise in his throat. He was sweating profusely with the fever but shivering uncontrollably with the cold. Jake had seen both of his parents die from the ague and knew what to expect. Charlie Owen wasn't long for this world

"He's asleep now. He's not in pain. We'd best let him rest and keep a vigil to see what happens."

"What do you think? Is he close to going?" Annie asked.

Jake shook his head sadly and looked down at his feet, avoiding eye contact with her. "I don't know. We can only watch and wait." He sat down with his back against the hut wall and signalled for the girl to sit beside him. Together they sat in silence, the quiet broken only by the laboured breathing of the old man on the bed. As the evening drew on they lit a fire and sat together in the light from the dancing flames. Neither of them bothered to eat or drink and they talked in low whispered voices. Charlie's condition did not dramatically alter but his breathing became shallower and more noisy.

"Will you leave the fens if they are drained?" Eventually Annie voiced the one question she had been dying to ask him.

Jake could hear the dread in her voice as she questioned him about his plans. He realised she had been through an awful period of loss, her son had died and now her father was dying. His heart went out to her and he hugged her closer to him. "Let's wait and see what happens about the drainage plans. I'm sure the slodgers will carry on their battle to stop them. I think we must face the present and let the future take care of itself." He kissed her lightly on her hair. "That much I learned in the army."

Annie snuggled up to him and covered her ears with her hands to cut out the sound of her father's laboured breathing. She had tried to be strong for her family but everything was closing in on her; her life felt so uncertain. She had been awake most of the previous night tending to her father and eventually fell asleep from sheer exhaustion. Jake sat still and held her in his arms as the fire died down and the night overtook them.

A short time after it got dark, Jake noticed a change in the old man's breathing. Charlie seemed to stop breathing altogether then took a few short breaths. This laboured pattern of respiration continued for a short time then the sounds of his breathing stopped altogether. Jake listened intently in the darkened shack for any signs of the old man reviving but he heard non and he knew Charlie Owen was dead.

An hour after Charlie took his last breath, his daughter woke up. She whimpered in the dark, temporarily unaware of where she was.

Jake spoke to her quietly and settled her panic. "You're alright, Annie. I have you safe."

She snuggled up to him and seemed to be about to go back to sleep, when she remembered her father. She sat upright and listened in the dark for signs of his breathing. Hearing non, she stood up, about to go to him to check on him but Jake held her back and wouldn't let go.

"He died while you were asleep. He went very peacefully. He just stopped breathing. He's better off now than he has been for years." Jake went over to the bed, closed Charlie's eyes and pulled up a blanket to cover his face.

Annie burst into sobs and buried her head in her hands. Jake could only hold her to comfort her. They spent that night huddled together, sitting against the hut wall facing the fire, sleeping fitfully for short periods. They were physically close but in their minds they were in far different places. Annie's thoughts were with her lost son and her dead father. Jake mulled over the events of the past twenty four hours and his future in the fens.

Next morning the priest was called and arrangements were made for the funeral. Annie became very quiet and withdrawn; she stopped crying and seemed to go into herself, busying herself with household chores and with making the eel traps and weaving nets. Jake was worried about her. This sudden change in her behaviour seemed out of character and was not at all what he had expected. He volunteered to move in with her until her father was buried.

"No. Thank you for the offer, but I must get used to being on my own and self sufficient." She looked so small and insignificant but her spirit was strong.

Jake nodded he understood, but resolved he would keep an eye on her and check regularly that she was alright and coping. Charlie Owen's body was moved to the church that day and Annie continued making her willow eel traps as if nothing had happened.

Jake needed time on his own to absorb the events of the last few days. He went onto the fen and checked all his traps. Being alone and away from people he had time to come to terms with the changes. Annie was on his mind quite a bit that day but she seemed to be coping far better than he had anticipated. Only time would tell if this acceptance of her fate was only bluff or if she really had such a strong spirit to ride out the storm.

Within a few days Charlie Owen was buried in Cubbit churchyard beside his wife and son. A few of the older members of the village joined Annie and Jake at the service in the little church. Charlie had been ill for so long many of his neighbours had forgotten he was still living amongst them.

Molly Kettle followed Annie to the churchyard gate after the funeral and stopped to speak with her, while Jake remained behind to thank the curate. "That's the last of them Annie. You're the only one left now. You've had it rough my girl. I am so sorry for you."

Annie managed a wan smile and thanked her for her concern.

Molly continued. "What will you do now?"

Annie brushed away a tear from her cheek. "I'll carry on making the willow eel traps and the nets as long as they are needed. It's the only life I know."

"What about Jake? Will he be here to support you?" Molly had noticed how close the pair had become.

Annie shrugged her shoulders. "He will leave Cubbit if the fens are drained. I don't know what will happen to me in the future."

Molly left the girl waiting for Jake to emerge from the church.

Jake eventually came out of the church but Annie could tell from his expression he was far from happy.

"What's happened? You don't look too pleased."

Jake ushered her through the churchyard gate and just shook his head. Once they were well away from the church and on their way home he explained. "Martin Somerscal was quizzing me about the wreckers. Someone has hinted I may be involved."

Annie looked askance at him. "Why would the curate question you? You're not involved are you?"

"No. I've not been on one of their raids yet."

She noticed his emphasis on that last word and dropped the subject.

Chapter Twenty Three

The investigation into Bert Ward's death was carried out at Spalding, his home town and the local administrative centre. The coroner's inquest was heard before a jury of twenty three local yeomen. The coroner in attendance, Mr. Thomas Cordle, called Lovell's overseer, as he was the first to find the body and questioned him at length. Jake was also ordered to attend the hearing as his gun was involved in the events of that night.

"As the overseer in charge of the Cubbit section of the drainage scheme, you must have seen much of the riots the night Bert Ward was killed."

"Yes sir."

"Did you hear the gun fire that night?"

"Yes sir, but I was too busy defending myself to take much notice of it."

"I understand you found the body, is that true?"

"Yes sir. I came on it first but Mr Lovell was just behind me."

"How do you think the Cubbit reeve met his death?"

"I've no doubt he was firing the gun when it blew up in his face, sir."

The coroner nodded. " Quite so. You may sit down."

After the overseer, the coroner called Jake to stand before him.

"You knew Bert Ward well, didn't you?"

Jake licked his lips nervously. "As well as anyone in Cubbit, Sir."

"Tell me about this firearm you owned."

"I brought it with me from my days with Robert Devereux's men, Sir. I fought alongside them in Ireland putting down Tyrone's rebellion. I was wounded with that gun and it was given to me as a trophy of war."

Thomas Cordle nodded and smiled at the young man. He was impressed by his manner. "You say it was stolen?"

"Yes Sir. I reported it to Ward as he was fen reeve at the time. I also reported it to the magistrates clerk here in Spalding."

The clerk pushed a piece of paper over the table to the coroner.

"Ah yes! I have the report here. So it was stolen from you but you don't know who stole it."

"No Sir. But in the circumstances I suspect it may have been Bert Ward."

"We have no way of proving that, however there's no denying the weapon came into his possession after you lost it."

Jake nodded agreement.

"You accused the dead man of shooting a young lad on a previous occasion. Can you explain that?"

Jake took a deep breath and chose his words carefully. "Toby Owen, a ten year old Cubbit boy was found shot at the same place that Ward was found dead. There are so few guns in the fens it can't just be a coincidence, Sir."

The coroner searched among the papers on the table before him. "I have the details of the enquiry into the boy's death. It was held at Cubbit. It seems he was killed by a shot to the chest but we have no way of saying who shot him and with what gun."

Jake nodded agreement.

Cordle continued. "You identified your gun at the scene of Ward's death. We have it here." He took the remains of the firearm from a bag at his side. "It seems the barrel of this gun exploded in Ward's face at the time he was trying to fire it."

Jake licked his dry lips again. "It would appear so."

"As a soldier experienced in the use of these firearms what do you think caused this explosion?"

Jake shook his head and shrugged his shoulders. "I can't be sure, Sir, but too much black powder would do it, or possibly some previous damage to the gun."

The magistrate consulted his notes once again. "Yes. It seems that is the general opinion. Dangerous things these matchlock guns. Tell me, did you have no trouble using it?"

"I hadn't used it, Sir. I had just had it repaired by the smith here in Spalding and hadn't a chance to use it before it was stolen."

That last statement seemed to satisfy the coroner. He waved his hand at Jake to sit down then ordered the jury to retire and consider their verdict.

The jury were not long in reaching their conclusion.. It was unanimously agreed that Bert Ward had caused his own death by firing a faulty gun.

The coroner recorded that Bert Ward's death was accidental and caused by his misuse of a firearm. In those circumstances no further action would be taken. There was no case to pass on to the Justices of the Peace for the area. Jake, who was the only living person to know the whole truth of the matter, was pleased the ordeal was over.

Bert Ward's funeral took place in Spalding, the town of his birth. He was buried in the churchyard in a family plot adjacent to the parish church. Most of Cubbit was pleased he had been removed from the locality and no one from the village, except his widow who had moved back to Spalding, attended his funeral.

Chapter Twenty Four

During the autumn months following Bert Ward's death, Lovell's drainage work continued. New banks were built, new dykes dug and new sluice gates fitted, but the slodgers continued their wrecking and the work made little real progress. Now opposition was much more organised. The drainage gangs never knew when to expect the next onslaught, so Lovell had to keep a strong presence of men on the river at all times. He had to dig deep into his fortune to try to save the drainage scheme, but his money was fast running out. In desperation, he arranged another meeting with Sir John Gamlyn at Fulney Hall.

Sir John was very civil to Lovell but not very helpful.

"Sit down, Thomas." Sir John poured his guest a glass of wine and sat down opposite to him. "We both know why you are here but I don't see what I can do for you."

Lovell shook his head, his mouth set in a hard line. "I am fast running out of money. These constant riots and the throwing down of my drainage works, have stretched my resources to the limit. I have wasted my entire fortune of £12,000 and still the work isn't done."

Sir John looked concerned. "I have approached all my contacts but no one is willing to lend you money. They all think the scheme is a lost cause. We are all concerned and shocked at the scale of the opposition."

Lovell slapped his knee hard with his fist. "I never met this problem in the low countries. A curse on these ignorant fen slodgers! Deeping fen will be the ruin of me."

Sir John nodded agreement but said nothing.

"Is there no hope of any financial help?" Lovell begged.

"I have spoken to Lord Burleigh and the Court of Sewers on your behalf. They have offered to increase your holding by a further 5,000 acres, once the scheme is completed, but there is no new money to be had."

Lovell shook his head. "That's like offering more water to a drowning man. If that's the best you can do, I'm afraid your drainage scheme is finished and I'm a broken man."

Sir John sat stoney faced and unmoved. In the beginning he had warned of some opposition to the scheme but he had anticipated nothing on the scale that Lovell had encountered. He knew the King had already lost interest in the area as there was no hope of immediate profit for the crown. Life could be hard, but at least he personally had lost nothing by trying. He spoke at last. "What will you do now?"

Lovell held his hands up in a gesture of defeat. "What can I do? Men will not work without pay. The high winter tides are due very soon and the fen will flood again as it always has. I am lost."

That winter Lovell's prediction came true. At the time of the highest tides, when there was a full moon, it coincided with heavy rainfall in the midlands. The extra volume of fresh water coming down the river, met the tidal salt water flowing inland, and the river banks were over run. They were breached in so many places the fen was inundated once again. The sldogers took the opportunity to remove all the remaining sluice gates and wind pumps so that the fen was returned to its former state and Lovell's drainage scheme became just a memory. All traces of the scheme vanished under the waves; it was as if it had never happened.

The Court of Sewers finally met at Stamford to consider their options. Thomas Lovell was summoned to appear before them. Lord Burleigh, who chaired the court, was cold and unsympathetic to Lovell's plight.

"The court has considered the situation. We have no choice but to remove our commission from you, Thomas Lovell. We must look to better men to undertake this great task." He made a note in the minutes of that meeting that Lovell's attempts to drain the Deeping fen were a failure owing to the 'unreasonableness of the times and riotous letts and disturbances of lewd people casting down the banks.'

Lovell, bankrupted and broken by the failure, could only hang his head in shame.

Life in the fens returned to its old rhythms. The slodgers fished and trapped eels, and netted wildfowl and ducks in season. It was as if Lovell's scheme had never been mooted.

Chapter Twenty Five

Jake Fowler continued his new way of life. He fished the rivers and the pools, and trapped the wildfowl, geese and ducks in season. His arrangement with Annie suited them both financially so they carried on with it.

Annie, left alone by the death of her son and then the loss of her father, worked every minute of her day to blot out the awful memories of her past. Jake slowly recovered from his ordeal in Ireland and the nightmares came less frequently. Left alone to get on with their separate lives they grew stronger and more self reliant. Things would probably have carried on like that indefinitely had Annie not fallen ill.

In the winter after Lovell's scheme was finally shelved, the cold weather came early. Frosts and snow covered the fens. Ice sealed the ponds and even the salt water of the river froze over. Jake struggled to catch his usual quota of eels and fish, and the wildfowl were driven from the fens to the coast in search of new feeding grounds. It was during this cold spell Annie fell ill.

The first Jake new of her predicament was when he called to get a damaged net mended. Annie was curled up in her bed, looking very pale and sick.

"What's happened to you?" Jake was concerned.

She sat up with difficulty and tried to answer him but her throat was so swollen she couldn't speak.

Jake threw down his damaged net and fetched some dried turf from the store behind the hut. He lit a fire to warm the room then looked around for something to cook for her to eat. From her appearance he guessed she hadn't eaten for a day or two and she was fast losing her strength.

"I'll go and fetch some bread and fish from my place, Annie. I wont be a minute." He sprinted back to his own home and collected what food he had. When he got back the fire was burning brightly and the hut had warmed up a little. Annie had shut her eyes and had pulled her single blanket up to her nose but she wasn't asleep. She smiled a wan smile at him as he bent over her to check on her.

"You're freezing cold." He held his hand against her forehead to feel her temperature. "I'll soon get you warm." He poked the fire, urging it into life. The flames leapt up into the cool air and sparks flew up towards the ceiling.

"I'll cook us a meal. You look as if you haven't eaten for days. You must eat to keep your strength up." He set about preparing the fish and making a stew.

Annie closed her eyes again and drifted off to sleep now that she was warm and cosy. Jake sat by the fire stirring the stew in the pot suspended over it and watching the sleeping girl.

When the meal was made, Jake took a bowl of it to Annie and fed her with it. She sat up in bed and managed to eat some of the stew and a few pieces of coarse bread dipped into it. Finally she pushed the bowl away and thanked Jake for feeding her. He sat back on the floor with his back against the hut wall and finished off the food. After eating, the girl drifted into a deep sleep.

By nightfall Annie was still fast asleep. Jake kept the fire in and made himself another meal before he prepared to go home to his own bed, but his plans didn't work out. Before he could leave her, Annie woke up delirious and in a fever. She ranted about her father and her lost son as if they were still alive. Jake could only stand by and soothe her sweating brow. She was burning up. He decided then he could not leave her and he must spend the night beside her, keeping the fire in and keeping an eye on her progress.

By morning, having spent an uncomfortable night sitting on the floor, Jake was stiff and tired. He had passed the night watching over Annie, listening to her ramblings and her cries. At first light he silently got up and left the hut to stretch his legs. Outside, the snow still lay thick on the roadway and icicles were forming on the edge of the rush thatch where the fire had melted the snow on the roof and the water had trickled down towards the ground. He broke off a long icicle and sucked on it to quench his thirst. He was looking out over the fen and wondering when he could hunt and fish again when he heard his name being called from inside the hut. Annie was awake and aware again. He went back into the hut to speak to her.

"Ah! You're with me again. It's nice to see you are recovering."

Annie smiled weakly at him and held out her hand.

Jake took her small hand in his and caressed it. She was no longer burning with a high temperature and seemed to be much more herself again.

"You look tired out." She said, trying to sit up in her bed.

Jake shook his head. "Stay where you are. Don't try to get up." He sat on the edge of her bed and tucked her blanket around her. "It's freezing outside. There has been more snow and by the looks of the sky there is more to come. You are in the best place."

She snuggled up to him and lay her head on his lap.

Warm and comfortable they both fell asleep. Annie from her exhausting illness and Jake from his sleepless night watching over her. Several hours later, he woke up to find the fire had almost burned out and the hut was going cold. Easing himself off the bed, he managed to extricate himself from her embrace without waking her, and made up the fire. The embers soon sprung into life when he added dry kindling and more turf. By the time Annie woke up again he had a good fire going and a pot of stew bubbling over it.

Annie recovered slowly from her illness. Jake had worried at first that she was developing the ague but as she recovered he realised it was a normal winter illness, probably brought on by the cold, the lack of food and the worry she had experienced losing her son and her father in such a short time. He was concerned about the girl and grew even fonder of her as he nursed her back to health.

After the first few difficult days, Jake felt she was recovering enough for him to go trapping and fishing again in the mornings. By then the snow had thawed, the ice had melted from the river and the wildfowl had returned to their feeding grounds on the marshes.

"I really must get back to hunting and trapping again, Annie. We will soon have no food and nothing to sell the kedger. Do you think you can manage if I just go out for the mornings?"

By early afternoon, when the winter light began to fail, he took his catch back to Annie's hut and made a meal for them both. Annie put a brave face on but it was obvious she would not cope if she was left on her own completely.

"I'll stay and keep an eye on you a few days more," Jake volunteered.

"In that case make a bed up on the opposite side of the hut, where my dad used to sleep. You can't sleep sitting against the wall any longer."

At the end of three weeks, Jake was pleased with her recovery and felt it was time to leave her and return to his own home but he was reluctant to go back on his own as he had grown accustomed to her company. But she seemed happy to go back to her solitary life.

Jake decided to spend one last night with Annie before he left her. He explained to her that as she was coping fine he felt he should return to his own home and his routine of fishing and trapping all day.

She didn't immediately reply to this suggestion and seemed preoccupied but finally she said. "Maybe you can spend one last night here before you go back home. I will miss you, you know." Jake was taken by surprise at this suggestion but willingly fell in with it.

That night after he'd made up the fire and banked it down with dampened turf to keep it burning all through the night, Jake said goodnight to Annie and curled up in his blanket to sleep. Tired from his day fishing on the river, he soon fell into a deep and dreamless sleep. Since the episode with Bert Ward and the gun, his nightmares had ceased. Facing up to his fears on that fateful night had finally laid to rest his demons and the memories of the shooting in Ireland.

At first light Jake woke up as usual but things were far from normal. He rolled over to find Annie cuddled up close to him and fast asleep. He felt for her under the bed cover and realised she was naked. He had no idea how long she had been there. At some time in the night she must have crept across the room and slipped into his bed. He lay there close to her and considered what to do; it was a new situation but one he was enjoying. He put his arm around her waist and pulled her closer to him.

Annie woke up soon after Jake. She made no attempt to get up from their shared bed but snuggled up to him. Emboldened by this show of affection, Jake bent over and kissed her. She put her arms around his neck and passionately returned the kiss.

"Do you still want to go and live alone?" She asked.

Jake grinned. "No, not if we can sleep like this every night."

She sighed and put her head on his chest. "I liked the look of you from the first day I saw you, Jake Fowler. I'm sorry it's taken me so long to get around to telling you."

He grinned even more. "I can say the same about you, Annie. You seemed so caught up in your busy life, struggling to bring up your son and nursing your dad, I didn't dare tell you."

"Are you still set on leaving the fens now the drainage scheme has failed?"

Jake smiled to himself. Why would he want to leave the area now. "No. I have all I could wish for. The fens are back as they should be and you are where you belong, with me."

They snuggled down together. All thoughts of leaving her and going onto the cold fen that day, were far from his mind. That could wait for another day.

The End

In 1632 work was again started to drain the Deeping Fen and turn it into rich agricultural land. This time the undertaking was successful.

Other Novels by this Author

Available from bookshops or direct from the publisher.
www.rexmerchant.co.uk   or   normancottage@yahoo.co.uk

St Anthony's Piglet.   ISBN 9781902474175

A medieval detective story set in the Lincolnshire fens during the reign of Edward I. At that period Spalding was ruled over by the head of the local Priory. It was a farming community with a thriving port used by fishermen and by merchants exporting woollen fleeces and importing wine, olive oil and woven wool cloth.

When Ivo Longspee, a Norman landowner related to the Earl of Lincoln, is found dead by poisoning, a young local fisherman is suspected of the crime.

Hugh Pinchbeck, a Spalding healer who had been a bowman on the crusades in his younger days, sets out to prove the young man's innocence.

The story unfolds at a time when King Edward is taxing his subjects heavily to finance his wars with the Scots and the Welsh.

The Runford Chronicles
A series of adult humorous fantasy novels

Book One - The Faerie Stone - ISBN 97819024740123

Book Two - The Tomatoes of Time - ISBN 9781902474007
*Winner of the Best Novel in the National Self-Publishing Awards
run by the Writers News.*

Book Three - The Pied Punch and Judy Man
ISBN 9781902474069

Book Four - The Archdruid of Macclesfield.
ISBN9781902474000

Book Five - Oswald Gotobed & the Cambeach Ghost.
ISBN 9781902474199

Published by
Rex Merchant

@
Norman Cottage

Contact us at
normancottage@yahoo.co.uk
www.rexmerchant.co.uk